Earl of the Marches

Cast in Time, Volume 5

Ed Nelson

Published by Eastern Shore Publishing, 2024.

Table of Contents

Dedication

THIS BOOK IS DEDICATED to my wife, Carol, for her support and help as my first reader and editor.

With special thanks to Ole Rotorhead for his technical insights on how things really work.

Then there are my beta readers: Ole Rotorhead, Lonelydad, Antti Huotari, Brent, Craig, and Don.

And never forget the professional editor, Janet E. Rupert

Quotation

"According to 'M' theory, ours is not the only universe. Instead, 'M' theory predicts that a great many universes were created out of nothing."

Stephen Hawking

Other books by Ed Nelson

The Richard Jackson Saga

Book 1: The Beginning
Book 2: Schooldays
Book 3: Hollywood
Book 4: In the Movies
Book 5: Star to Deckhand
Book 6: Surfing Dude
Book 7: Third Time is a Charm
Book 8: Oxford University
Book 9: Cold War
Book 10: Taking Care of Business
Book 11: Interesting Times
Book 12: Escape from Siberia
Book 13: Regicide
Book 14: What's Under, Down Under?
Book 15: The Lunar Kingdom
Book 16: First Steps

In the Richard Jackson World

Mary, Mary
More Mary

Stand Alone Story

Ever and Always

The Cast in Time series

Book 1: Baron
Book 2: Baron of the Middle Counties
Book 3: Count
Book 4: Earl
Book 5: Earl of the Marches

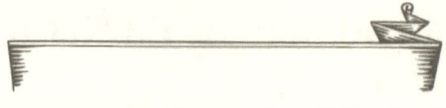

Copyright © 2024

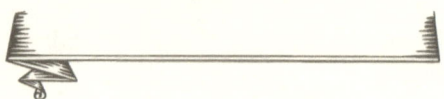

E. E. Nelson
All rights reserved
Eastern Shore Publishing
2331 West Del Webb Blvd.
Sun City Center, FL 33573

ISBN 979-8-89434-006-7
Library of Congress Control Number: 20239124

Chapter 1

Now that we had conquered the Franks and began to absorb them into our culture, an immediate problem resulted from our victory.

We now had a border with the Gauls. They were related to the Celts and could communicate with many of our people.

This territory was the area that would become known as Germany. The Gauls were an expansionist group due to pressure from the Slav tribes. Broken into small tribes, they could be handled easily. Once one of the tribes became dominant, they would be a handful.

Our ability to communicate with them was another opportunity for us to change their culture.

Unfortunately for me, there was a dominant tribe at our northern border. This area would become Alsace-Lorraine in the future. Alsace-Lorraine would be the site of many future battles between modern France and Germany. The area is rich in coal and iron ores, which were a constant bone of contention.

I wasn't ready for a battle with the Gauls then, so I had to stabilize our mutual border to avoid war.

By stabilizing the border, I meant making it so strong they wouldn't dream of crossing it. Sure, they could dream of crossing our border but not do it.

Our common border was too long to build a wall along its length. At least all at once.

We had done this enough that my people had it down to a science. First, we kept a large army stationed along the border to prevent incursions while we built our defenses. This tactic was countered by the Gauls stationing troops on their side of the border.

The only difference was that we understood logistics and the need to provide food to our army. The Gauls were still at the point where they lived off the land.

Living off the land worked for an army on the march, not for a stationary army. They soon had killed off all the deer and wild pigs in their area. They had to go farther and farther to keep their men fed. Any farmer in their area had long fled, leaving little in their wake.

On the other hand, we cut roads immediately so supplies could be brought to the new front. In some cases, we were able to rehabilitate old Roman roads. Our front lines had been laid out. Along the frontier, we had a series of forts built. At first, they were nothing but rough camps built like the old Roman marching camps.

As soon as one of these camps was ready for occupancy, we started on a more permanent version within a few days. Our forts could withstand anything less than cannon fire with double-wide concrete walls and watch towers.

Inside the walls, we built standard barracks and support buildings. We also added oversized warehouses. The idea was to have more than enough food to feed our people and provide the Gauls with food if needed.

I wanted to be a good neighbor while being prepared to fend off attacks.

The surveyors started laying out the roads and railroad paths to connect Paris to the northern border. There would be three main roads and main lines out of Paris. There would be several roads crisscrossing so traffic could be diverted from one location to another as needed.

While the physical stuff was underway, we also opened a dialog with the chieftains along the way. We wanted the local Franks to benefit from what we were doing and to influence the Gauls on our border.

We ensured that our Franks were well fed and had MASH units visit them to address health problems. Baroness Agnes had started with a single mobile hospital. She now had one hundred of them fully staffed and working our country and our allies.

They moved freely about the country. We always sent a guard contingent along, but it was woe to anyone who attacked a MASH unit. They were hailed as miracle workers everywhere they went, and to attack them was madness. The locals would hunt them down and kill them to a man. It only took a couple of times, and the units were sacrosanct.

All along our border with the Gauls, we sent teams to upgrade their food and grain storage and improve their roads and MASH units to help with their health care.

We also provided radio sets to every village. They could receive and transmit. They were told we would respond if they were attacked and to call us. These were for communication. We also provided battery-powered receiving units so they could listen to our music programs.

The batteries could be exchanged for new or recharged ones at the many trading posts we established along the border. We kept them fully stocked with a full range of goods as usual; mirrors were the most sought-after items. The next items sought after were small telescopes.

We even set up photography studios at each marketplace. For a very small fee, we would take pictures of anyone requesting it.

Since we had a tavern at each trading post, we had the normal amount of drunken rowdiness. Drunks were thrown in the drunk tank for the night and released the next morning. We took their fingerprints and pictures to start a database of troublemakers.

Most were innocent farm boys out on the town for the first time. Others were thieves and troublemakers. We also had a guest registry at each marketplace. Our "guests" were entered into the census database we were starting on the Gauls.

In Vietnam, we called it hearts and minds. The only difference was that we had a chance of it working here. The Gauls were segmented into so many tribes that they were always in a low-conflict situation with each other. As such, there was no organized insurgency.

We met with the local chiefs in each area and made agreements with them. We would defend them from open incursions if they didn't attack us. It was understood if they raided another tribe, they were on their own as far as self-defense.

That plan worked about half the time. There was always something stirring between the tribes along the border. That was fine with me as long as they left us alone.

Only once did we have to send in troops to retrieve our citizens, who had been seized in a raid. They would have been sold as slaves further into Gaul. The village warriors thought they could resist and paid the price. Once our people were safe, we leveled the village. No woman and children were harmed directly, but they were left without food and shelter.

Pax Cornwall was a harsh pax.

We had twenty thousand troops to secure the border with fifteen hundred cannons in support. Two thousand of the troops were mounted cavalry.

As the roads were built, the track beds for our trains were laid. These were the first tracks with four feet eight and a half inches between them. This width was the United States standard gauge. We had developed steam locomotives that were Atlantic class 4-4-2 engines. With that, we could haul full-sized railcars.

We instituted the first in France since there were no tracks in place. A replacement program was underway in all Cornish territories, but it would take years to implement.

In a bit of nostalgia, I had the box cars labeled forty and eight. They could haul more, but it seemed fitting for me to use that marking in France.

While all this was happening, I realized it was time to start on another level of invention. Maybe we were ready for the vacuum tube to improve our lighting and radio system. Developing a working light bulb would take a lot of trial and error. Though I knew what Edison and his technicians had gone through, it would still be a chore.

With all that going on, you would think I wouldn't have time for my family. It was just the opposite. I finally had a bureaucracy set up that could handle the day-to-day affairs of Cornwall. The military was operating under the command of their officers, and the officers were supported by a staff similar to that of the Pentagon.

The only difference was that our "Pentagon" staff officers had to buy in for any changes the field officer corps wanted. The Pentagon, in turn, couldn't force changes on the field officers, only make suggestions. This policy left the ones at the sharp end in control of their fate.

We now had an Army, Navy, Marine Corps, and Air Force. The Air Force primarily comprised observation balloons, but work was ongoing to manufacture large dirigibles for long-distance flights and heavy lifting. Heavier than air flight was a long way away. The biggest drawback was finding a source of helium to replace the dangerous hydrogen. The only one I knew of was in what was to become Texas.

Hydrogen could be used, but it was extremely dangerous if not handled correctly. We would have to develop a lightweight internal combustion engine before developing lighter than air transport. There would be a long wait.

The army had developed a steam-driven tank corps. I didn't have much hope for them except on a set-piece battlefield. They were rattling, clanking monsters that broke down every five miles. I only let them be put into service to allow a battlefield doctrine to be developed. We would need it when we developed the diesel engine.

Tom and I had many arguments over the usefulness of these monsters. He envisioned them leading our troops to victory across Europe. I envisioned them broken down or mired in mud.

He pushed his people into building more reliable machines. This practice did help with our overall manufacturing program, as tighter tolerances helped us all the way around.

We also had a "state department", which was charged with diplomatic relations with the other countries in our orbit. Their staff was chosen from the ranks of officers who had served in those countries. I wouldn't have a group of new students decide my foreign policy.

That has always caused problems in the US government. As a former military officer, I knew I was biased, but I'd had to clean up too many of their failed policies.

I also kept a tight rein on any CIA off-the-books wars under my watch. Those were other messes I had to help clean up.

It was a grand and glorious day when I opened our new postal service's first post office. We now had enough educated people to make smooth white paper so that people could send letters to each other.

My picture was on the one penny stamp, the most common usage. Eleanor is on the highest-value stamp. Hers was a one silver stamp which could mail a twenty-pound parcel. We hadn't set a weight limit on what could be shipped, but I clarified that no drunks could be mailed home.

Chapter 2

In addition to carrying out my self-appointed duties, I went through another exercise that I seemed to do every year.

I asked myself, *Why am I here, and how did I get here?*

By here, I mean in the body of a young baron in eighth-century Cornwall. I know I died in my sleep and woke up here, but some mechanism had to make the transfer.

Was it God? I'm not even certain I ever believed in God, so why me? Was it a random chance thing in this universe? I had read a little about what Einstein called spooky action at a distance or quantum mechanics. If so, what triggered it?

Being here with my knowledge appeared to be more than a random chance. If it wasn't random chance, then there was a reason I was here. Why wasn't I made aware of the reason?

I had to be in an alternate reality or what would be an alternate reality to my beginning point in the future. That had to be true, whether triggered by God or random chance. I was reluctant to think it was a random chance because of my background and the knowledge I carried in my head.

Even that might not be true. Maybe many thousands or millions of other people died and were awakened to this reality. Most would have failed to survive their first day on this path.

It was a brute force method, but the keyword was a method. That ruled out random chance, or at least I thought it did.

I prayed to the God I didn't believe in and wasn't surprised when I didn't get an answer. Maybe he or she didn't believe in me.

I couldn't think of any experiments I could run to prove either point. Even if I could prove it was God or chance, what good would it do? I was here and had to make the best of it as I could. I was the one defining the best of it.

If it were random chance, it would explain why I didn't have an overriding direction. If it was God, why could I do what I wanted? I know about free will and all that, but this was taking it to an extreme.

As with every other year, I couldn't arrive at any answers or even a theory that would hold water. I could only live on my terms and let it play out.

If it was random chance, I was left with all I could do was live my life. If it were God, all I could do was live my life.

I reach this conclusion every year. Maybe I could let it go next year and just live my life.

After my annual bout of introspection, I got back to work.

I wanted a mindless enterprise to clear my head, so I called my team of scribes together and started dictating every book I had ever read about light bulbs and vacuum tubes. There weren't very many.

Once the books had been transcribed and the paper copies turned over to the print shop, I went to our new engineering school and spoke to the dean.

I needed to assemble a team for the tube and bulb project. I asked the dean for recommendations for team members. I told him they had to be familiar with electricity and glass making.

The dean came up with a list of five students. She had three people who concentrated on electricity and two glass experts.

The glass people came from families specializing in making glass and majored in the subject. The electricians were the highest ranked in their class on the subject.

I quizzed her about the different team members that she had submitted. They may be experts in their field but had to learn to work together as a team.

After discussing the various team members, we decided that one of the electricians had too much ego to integrate into the team. The next person on her list was knowledgeable and considered easy-going, so we went with him.

The proposed team members were invited to a meeting at the keep. I wanted to see how they interacted, and I had them set up in a separate room. The reception room had nice furniture and was provisioned with plenty of snacks and various drinks.

Once they were assembled at the correct time, I had word sent that I would be an hour late and for them to go ahead and enjoy the drinks and snacks comfortably.

Being the rotten person I am, I had two people listening and watching them through peepholes.

It didn't take long for things to sort themselves out. These were all guys, so there was no sexual interplay.

Four of them gathered refreshments and talked about what the subject of this meeting was about.

The fifth guy, a glassmaker, decided to take advantage of the free food and drink, especially the drink. He also began picking on the youngest man present, saying that his being there was an obvious mistake.

We had two people waiting in the wings without knowing they would replace any who failed our little test. I had both of them sent in to join the group and had the drinker pulled out for a brief meeting. His meeting was brief. He was handed ten silver and thanked for his time.

I followed him out of the building, where he promptly went to the nearest sports Tav and spent his ten silver on more drinks.

The two new members of the team, a glassmaker and an electrician, settled in nicely with the group and waited for my arrival.

Giving them another half an hour with nothing going amiss, I entered the room and explained what I wanted from them.

The financial achievements of previous successful teams were well known, so you could feel the excitement in the room when I announced their opportunity.

Their first assignment was to review the books I had dictated. They were then to devise a working plan to include a budget, the infrastructure required, and a timeline.

I assured them that none of their original projections would work out, but they needed to start somewhere. I also informed them what their starting salaries would be so they could plug that into the budget. They were a happy crew who departed my conference room to start to work.

I had to chuckle; in their initial excitement, they hadn't determined where to hold their first meetings. Since they had all split up to let their families know their good news, it would be interesting to see who would take things under control and be the team leader.

Another item that had to be taken care of was the drunk. The drunk would realize why he had been kicked off the team. He could go either way. He could sober up and go straight or drink himself to death and cause problems for everyone along the way.

He had talent, so I decided to try to save him. I had Baroness Agnes' people approach him with his parents' support. They put him in a rehab group. This group wasn't a voluntary one. It was like being in prison until you dried out.

After that, he would be counseled and exercised to get himself into shape. He would be offered a job in Arette, which could always use a technical person if he got through that. This move would put him far from the bulb team to avoid problems.

I knew that the bulb team would make good progress to a point. The team would have no problem manually creating bulbs by blowing them into a molten bulb of flint glass.

We could use carbon filaments made from bamboo and could make the bottom portion as an Edison screw. Assembling one bulb and drawing a vacuum with a special pump would be a chore with many failures, but it could be done.

These would be handmade light bulbs with a life expectancy of one thousand hours, which would be proof of concept. The issues would arise when they tried to mass-produce bulbs. It would be interesting to watch how they proceeded. I figured introducing the light bulb for daily use would take five or more years.

While my soul-searching and team-building continued, my life as a leader of a burgeoning power continued.

In Spain, the Moors finally woke up to the fact that we were in Gibraltar to stay and took umbrage at our possession of the rock.

While Gibraltar had always been a landmark, it had never been a fortified position that could block the Mediterranean from the Atlantic. Our cannons changed the equation.

The Moors kept attacking our positions at the base of the rock, but we had built solid walls that couldn't be tipped over and had plenty of cannon embrasures. With watch towers and balloons, we always had warnings that the enemy was approaching, so we had forces in place to defend.

With telescopes and the rock's elevated position, they couldn't even sneak up on us overnight.

I had my general staff planning an invasion of Hispaniola. Spain, in this world, had not been unified yet. We would have to fight five different groups to control the country I thought of as Spain.

Aragon, Catalonia, Navarre. Asturias Leon, and Al Andalus. I hadn't made up my mind about the Balearic Islands yet.

We might get lucky, and the first four on my list that comprised the northern portion of Spain would join together, and we could fight them all at once. The Visigoths didn't have a history of cooperation, so I didn't get my hopes up.

The first decision that had to be made was the invasion route. There were passes through the Pyrenees that could be used, but I was reluctant to go through Basque territory without their cooperation. Thus, the first item on the list was to send a delegation to the Basque to see if they would let us through their territory and what the price would be.

If they said no or the price was too high (like our weapons), our invasion would be by sea, opening up a whole can of worms. With the Moorish invasion, which was going on, it would be complex.

This complexity would especially be true when we got to Al Andalus. We might be fighting the Visigoths one day and then fighting beside them against the Moors the next.

If we invaded by sea, the best port to use would be the harbor of what would be Santander. The area was an extension of the Basque territory, but they would have to live with it. Since it wasn't as mountainous, we could fight them.

Portugal hadn't emerged as a separate political identity. Normally, it would take another two hundred years to settle out. I didn't intend to let the separation between it and Spain develop.

One, I didn't want the headache of another country to rule, and two, the minerals in Portugal were plentiful. At the same time, they had no iron, coal, or aluminum. They did have tin, tungsten, copper, and even gold. Uranium was also to be found there, but I hoped it would be a long time before we needed that.

My generals recommended a two-prong approach. Start negotiations with the Basques and develop a presence in Santander.

That made sense to me, so we contacted the Basques, and our trading ships started calling on Santander. We didn't take long to negotiate with Catalonia to buy land for a trading post. Since we weren't Greek, the Catalonia leaders weren't wary of us bearing gifts.

We kept our prices low and paid high bribes, so there were no objections as we volunteered to improve the harbor so larger ships could call. With a better harbor, it made sense that we bought more land and erected warehouses.

Since it was a nice climate compared to Cornwall, several mansions were built by some of our prominent families to make things look less suspicious. As I say, beware of Cornish men bearing gifts.

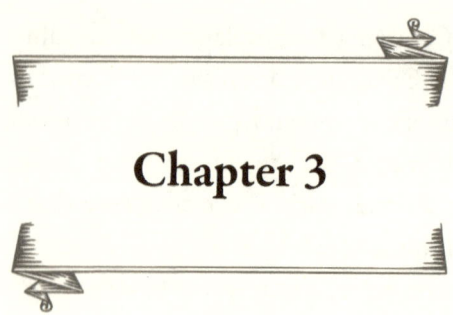

Chapter 3

We had set up trading posts along our border with the Gauls. We expanded on that concept by allowing them to sell goods at the trading post. In effect, we now had markets in place of our stores.

Our merchants had to pay a small fee to set up a wooden stall in the main marketplace. They were also allowed to sell in an open field adjacent to the market using blankets on the ground with no fees.

The market was created to encourage all of the Gauls to feel free to join us. An unintended consequence was that not only poor families used the free space, but widows and orphans took advantage of this opportunity.

In turn, we took the opportunity to provide health care for everyone who showed up. Not only that, but a school was also started to teach elementary reading, writing, and mathematics for free to any who wanted to stay longer. Naturally, it was our language that was taught.

That was easier than we had feared since we discovered that the Gauls were ethnically and linguistically similar to Cornishmen and could communicate on a basic level without additional language instruction.

Our teachers were on the lookout for fast learners and natural leaders. These were given discreet support by providing them with a mentor. The mentors were mostly our soldiers along the border who wanted to pick up some extra money for providing advice to the ones who would be the future local leaders of the Gauls tribes.

We kept a close eye on the mentors. Any abuse was quickly and forcibly stopped. We didn't want to alienate this group of future leaders. The idea behind this program was the same as the Green Berets of my time. We wanted to win their hearts and minds.

We had one huge advantage: no VCs or their local equivalent were trying to sabotage our efforts. Unlike the Peace Corps, we didn't do things for them; we taught them, and it was their choice if they wanted to use the knowledge.

We called the fast learners and the potential leaders the Future Ones. This term was used only in our internal meetings.

This group was taught the basics of math and literacy and how to keep a village or farm clean. These demonstrations included showing them microbes with a microscope and why a sewage system and cleanliness were necessary.

If they requested, their mentor would accompany them to their homes to help them identify what they needed to do and how to do it. Again, we weren't doing it for them, just showing them what they had to do. We wanted a stronger Gaul, but stronger on our terms. If they could pull themselves up by their bootstraps, they wouldn't look at us with envious eyes.

It didn't take us long to realize that our mentors had to have schooling on building a septic system and/or improving food storage.

The next thing you know, we were using the mentoring system to identify our future leaders in the military. So not only were courses included in our mentoring schools on improving Gaul's infrastructure, but now there were leadership classes.

We didn't have a mentor school at every marketplace. These were held at each keep along the border. As our need for mentors grew, we increased class size and frequency until the schools became a permanent fixture, and attendance was required for advancement in the armed services. We now had NCO schools!

The teaching of mentors and the Future Ones worked so well that we instituted them along our borders and in every one of our territories. This teaching was even offered to Iceland, who accepted gladly. They had seen what we had achieved in their many trading missions with us and wanted the same.

Berets weren't a known headwear, but anyone who passed the mentoring school was given a green flash to wear on their right shoulder. This patch was the first of the specialties that formed what we called uptime, the Tower of Power.

I had mentioned that the mentors mostly came from our armed forces. Some of them were civilians. We welcomed anyone who could pass our basic literacy tests and an interview about their suitability to be a mentor.

There weren't many of these, but they were fast-tracked on project teams and local planning groups. The military was requiring their NCOs to attend and pass the mentoring school. We soon had a class of jobs of preferred civilians who passed the courses.

Without advertising our program, the general population caught on to this program. It soon became a competition for admittance to the schools.

This competition concerned me as the political types soon pressured me to have their recommendation given preference on admission. I came down heavy on this practice. Even local headmen and barons were charging the prospective students for their recommendation.

Two hangings stopped that practice.

I only reviewed the high-level concepts of the mentoring program and the mentoring schools. They were the product of my local leaders. This turn of events was thrilling as we had the beginnings of a meritocracy. I wasn't foolish enough to think it would be a pure system, but anything was better than inherited power, except for my children.

The army was the first to adopt the mentoring program, which was now renamed the NCO school. The Navy and Air Force weren't far behind. For the Navy, it was more of a true NCO school as they didn't have many opportunities for local mentoring.

The Air Force, still comprised of observation balloons, taught their future NCOs and gave balloon ascensions to the locals along whichever border they were assigned. These ascensions didn't do much in creating infrastructure but went a long way in convincing people they would have difficulty fighting us. The balloon people were wise enough to stack the deck. They only took up their students on the clearest and calmest days to demonstrate how far one could see with a telescope.

At five hundred feet with no mountains or hills in the way, one could see twenty-six miles with the naked eye. They had tripod-mounted thirty-six power telescopes in the balloons, so it was easy to impress the students. An ascension even impressed me with the equipment they were using.

On an ascension I made from one of the border keeps, I spied a field covered with yellow flowers so thick it appeared to be painted a rich yellow from a distance. A few questions led to the discovery that this was rapeseed, which was generally regarded as a weed in my domains because its oil and seed meal were considered inedible.

Botany and nutritional science had not been an area of concentration for me, but I remembered two things about rapeseed oil that gave me pause. One was that it could be used both as a lubricant and as a fuel, both for engines and for lamps. The other was that by reducing via selective breeding the proportion of oil and seed that were contaminated with erucic acid, it could be made edible both by people and by livestock! It had been marketed as "canola oil".

Even better, it thrived in northern Europe and Britain and made a good winter cover crop for a spring harvest. It could provide a concentrated fuel for lamps and steam engines right now, for diesel in the near future, and also serve as a lubricant, and one of these days might be a useful cooking oil and seed meal livestock feed.

Of immediate utility, it made a stable and efficient fuel for hot air balloons so that we could dispense with the difficult-to-produce hydrogen and the impossible-to-find helium!

During all this, some actions were happening on the home front. I didn't pay a whole lot of attention when Eleanor asked me a few questions about the women's clothes referred to in some of the romances I had dictated.

I didn't pay attention at first, anyway. The second time my wife asked, I wondered what was going on. The third time, I knew there was something afoot.

I found out soon enough when mother and daughter appeared in my office. Both were wearing the cutest sun dresses. I told them they could have come straight out of one of the fashion magazines I had read while waiting in many a doctor's office or at Dorry's bedside in her last illness.

Eleanor wore a white dress with a pattern of red roses. Cathy's was yellow with daisies. The most astonishing thing was they were made out of cotton!

I stuttered a bit. I was torn between complimenting the dresses and their looks and asking them where the material came from.

Luckily for me, the compliments came out first.

"You both look wonderful in those dresses. They are identical to what a woman would wear in the summer in my time. The dresses are almost as beautiful as the ones wearing them."

That earned me large smiles and a curtsey from both ladies.

"Where did you get the material? The only source of cotton that I know of is Egypt."

Eleanor answered, "A Byzantine trading ship brought the cotton. I was fortunate enough to be at the docks while it was being unloaded. I was curious about the material, and when I examined the weave, I knew it was the material referred to in some of the romances.

"I bought all the bolts of material and had these dresses cut from a pattern you helped me with."

"I knew something was up when you asked about the cut of sun dresses in romances. I never thought that you might be able to get cotton fabric."

"This fabric is delightful. It isn't as heavy as wool, so it will be cooler in the summer. It isn't as rough as linen, so it is more comfortable. I'm having underclothes made using this miracle cotton fabric."

Cathy piped up, "Mother will make a fortune selling the rest of the cotton she bought."

"How much did you buy?"

"A thousand bolts that are two yards wide and ten yards long. I expect to get ten gold a bolt."

"That is a lot of money."

Eleanor continued, "I told the captain of the trading ship that I would buy all that he could bring me. I had to pay two gold a bolt for these but negotiated the full load down to one and a half gold per bolt."

"Good work, my dear," I praised her.

"Thank you. Now, what about these fashion magazines you mentioned?"

Dang, I knew I was in trouble as soon as the words came out of my mouth. I had hoped she had forgotten.

I gave in to the inevitable and told her about fashion magazines. I did keep it to fashions and descriptions of what was in style. I didn't want to read articles on improving your love life. Or how to cope when your boyfriend dumped you, or how to dump that inconvenient boyfriend.

I had to promise that I would dictate some of those magazines. That gave me a headache thinking about it. How would I dictate drawings? I could do an engineering draft easily. Fashion plates, not so much.

When I explained that difficulty after tearing up fifty different attempts, an artist was assigned to me, I would roughly explain the dress and its particular function, such as daily wear, cocktails, professional, and the hundred other types of dresses women wore.

I learned to regret mentioning cocktails as I soon had to give out the recipes for dozens of drinks. Then, to top it all off, I used the term cocktail party in the presence of Eleanor. We had a cocktail party and hors d'oeuvres almost every Saturday evening while I was at the keep.

These hors d'oeuvres included appetizers like meatballs, deviled eggs, pinwheels, and pigs in a blanket.

I thought I had escaped pigs in a blanket forever. I hated those things. The only things worse at the cocktail parties were the inane conversations or the attempts to lobby me on various projects that would benefit the lobbyist. Someone never brought up a project that would benefit all in the land rather than their interests.

I took to disappearing halfway through these events. After an almost terse conversation with Eleanor, she saw my point and eased up on the party frequency. Still, it was a horrid three months until she reduced the parties to once a month.

I thought I was home free until the invitations started coming in for parties at other houses and Keeps. A reporter had been invited to one of our parties. Accidentally, I'm certain.

The next news issue contained a detailed description of the party. The food, the drink, and the ladies' apparel were included, not only the attendees.

Since our newspaper had a worldwide distribution, well within our zone of influence at least, I could see the Byzantine Emperor having to introduce cocktail parties to his court. That alone would be enough reason for him to declare war on us.

At the same time, I had to chuckle at the thought of the Mongols getting a copy. That could set off a world war.

Chapter 4

The new fashions took our countries by storm. Every woman with any ambition wanted one of the dresses in the new fabric.

The bolts that Eleanor had bought had to be rationed as some women wanted to buy dozens of them. Eleanor knew this would create a class war, making the baron's fights look like child's play.

Nothing was worse than a bunch of women fighting over a bolt of cloth. I remember Black Fridays and George Washington Birthday Day sales from uptime. Staid women who would never do anything out of line devolved into hair-pulling harridans. It was awesome and revolting at the same time.

There weren't enough bolts for every woman to have one. Eleanor solved this using elementary arithmetic. She had a scribe examine how many women were in each census area. It worked out that we had about five hundred thousand women in our territories and other allies.

She held a lottery in each area. Ten thousand bolts and five hundred thousand women worked out to one in fifty women getting a bolt in the lottery she held in each area.

These lotteries were big deals. The drawings were broadcast over the radio stations. The local troops guarded the bolts. The drawings were as secure as the acting award's uptime. No one could fix the well-guarded bowls with all the women's names and addresses.

Even so, there were lawsuits after the drawings by other women with the same names. These were given short shrift in the local courts.

Once the bolts were distributed, another problem arose. What type of dress to make was the big question, and where could they get a pattern to follow?

Eleanor and her staff had thought this through. They had a catalog of the different dress styles and a description of the occasion for which the dress should be worn, the time of year it was seasonable, and what designs worked with each dress.

Explanations about vertical and horizontal stripes and floral design sizes were included.

The catalog listed what pattern should be ordered to cut the fabric correctly with each type of dress. Explanations of dress sizes and how to measure them were included.

Dress sizes led to many wails of anguish as some realized they wore small sizes. In our world at this time, a size twelve was considered perfect. Their friends pitied those poor ladies who wore a size eight or lower. The poor people's chances of a good marriage were lessened.

Eleanor and I didn't need the money, so she donated all the funds from the catalog and patterns to various charities. These charities were listed in the catalog, and people could check where they wanted their money sent.

It was an excellent public relations move on Eleanor's part. She made a fortune off the bolts of fabrics but improved her image with the lottery and donations to charity. No one ever questioned the hundred bolts she reserved for the ladies of the keep.

A much more serious event happened while all this nonsense was going on.

We received a radio report from our base at the mouth of the Niger River. There was an outbreak of a devastating disease. From the symptoms described, it was either Ebola, Marburg, or some other hemorrhagic fever.

An exploration party from upstream returned to the settlement. Within two weeks, the first symptoms were reported in the settlement. These were fever, muscle pain, headaches, and sore throats.

Shortly after that, people developed vomiting, diarrhea, rashes, and decreased kidney function. Next, people started to bleed externally. From the bruising being reported, there was also internal bleeding.

The settlement had four hundred and fifty people. Of that, over two hundred died. Those who recovered were weakened for a long time, some for the rest of their lives.

From start to finish, the fever ran its course twelve days after the first symptoms were noted. It was terrible being thousands of miles away and unable to do anything but recommend keeping the patients hydrated as much as possible.

There were IV kits to pump fluids, but we never expected to need so many. The hospital ran out on the second day. All they could do was get the patients to drink the boiled water or twist a wet rag over their lips.

The worst thing for me was knowing the disease family and not being able to do anything about it. Even uptime, it wasn't easy to control.

We sent medical help with hundreds of IV kits, but it was too late. What was sad were the last messages sent from those who had contracted the disease.

We instituted a quarantine procedure for those who went out of the settlement to explore. It worked as there was never a problem again, but once more, I should have foreseen this event.

We even moved the settlement away from the riverbank. Of course, the docks and associated warehouse had to be left alone, but housing was moved to higher dry ground.

We also made DDT since we could produce chlorobenzene from our petroleum distillates. We used this liberally around our settlement at the docks and the housing.

I know all about the dangers of DDT but felt that since we wouldn't be using as much on the scale that uptime agriculture had, the risks were worth it.

I didn't want my people to die from something I could have prevented. When it came down to it, I think Ben Franklin had selected the right bird. I thought I was being funny with that thought but quickly realized it was not a laughing matter.

We would use DDT but work on other methods of mosquito control. We drained and filled low areas where water could gather to prevent the creation of mosquito breeding grounds.

Those terrible twelve days of our people suffering and dying were broadcast on public radio. I had to decide if I wanted the whole event kept secret or to let the whole world know what was happening.

An event of this magnitude could never be kept quiet for long, so on day one, I let the colony's broadcast go wide. My advisors recommended against it, but I had seen what the result of a coverup could lead to.

If you were looking for ratings, this event recorded the highest ever. We allowed the colony's broadcasts to be shared over the open air and added our responses and actions to the program.

Archbishop Luke ordered extra masses at all churches. He wasn't trying to boost his attendance; he genuinely believed the prayer would help.

The news people interviewed relatives of those in Africa. Some were angry, but most were hopeful. Each day, the death toll was announced along with the deceased names. To say it was a grim time was putting it mildly.

I was castigated in op-eds for allowing this to happen. Other editorials defended me. If my position were elected, my seat would have been in jeopardy during the next elections.

After the fever had burnt out, I ordered a cenotaph to be erected in the colony with the names of all who died engraved on the front. On the back were the names of those who had fought the disease, with an asterisk denoting those whose health was permanently damaged.

I started a fund to support those who couldn't work anymore. My people also contributed. The fund grew so large we had to make it a common disaster fund; otherwise, people would have lived far beyond their previous standard of living.

Eleanor told me I had to leave town a month after things settled down. I hadn't slept regularly for weeks, and my body showed it.

I rode with my escort to the silver mine at the base of Mt. Brunwenely. It was remote enough for me to relax without people coming to me in the street to voice their opinions.

My excuse was that I hadn't visited the mine in some time. The mine didn't need a visit from me, but I needed a reason to get away. It was going to take us three days to get there. I could have taken the train that now ran to the mine, but I wanted to take my time and relax.

The trip wasn't exactly roughing it. My tent was also a mobile headquarters with a separate bedroom, living area, and conference room. Another tent contained our radio communications.

I would never be allowed out alone or without contact with the world again. I was okay with that as long as every little problem wasn't brought to me. My staff was good, and I hadn't had a message in three days.

The silver mine knew we were coming, so they cleaned the place. That meant there were no tailings lying around to trip over. The mine was still a strip mine as the ore vein was clustered near the surface.

Test drillings had been made so they knew the ore-bearing silver continued for over a mile. Estimates were that the vein was over fifty yards thick. That was a lot of silver.

I was shown around the area, and at the end of the day, I congratulated all on a job well done and encouraged them to keep up the good work. As I said, the visit was an excuse to escape the aftermath of the African disaster.

I realized that I'm not God and couldn't make it a perfect world. Still, I was bothered by the loss of life when it might have been prevented. Hindsight is 20/20, as they say.

They even said it now in this time period. Our eyeglasses were still selling well in our marketplaces. I may have used the term once or twice and now it was in common usage.

We started back early one morning. I wanted to prolong this trip as much as possible, so I still didn't take the train. No new emergencies were reported, so I didn't have to feel guilty about taking my time.

The second evening on the trip home, I was eating dinner at our campfire when I noticed movement near my feet.

At first, I couldn't figure out what type of animal it was. Once I had it in focus, I realized it was an Irish wolfhound pup.

Its fur was all matted as though it hadn't been cared for in a long time, if ever. It was small and was nothing but skin and bones. You could count its ribs.

It crawled to me subserviently and wagged its tail while licking its chops. The poor thing was near starvation. I threw a small piece of the roast boar from our dinner this evening.

To say it wolfed it down would be an understatement. As it ate, I got a better look at the dog. The pup was all male. He couldn't have been over several months old, just past being weaned.

How he got here was beyond me. It looked like a purebred, and they were worth a lot of money. How it ended up in the middle of nowhere was anyone's guess.

It continued to beg for food, and I fed him one small slice at a time. One of my men brought over a dish of water, which the pup promptly lapped dry. This dog would have died in a few days if we hadn't come along.

When I finished, I let him lick my plate clean. He then flopped down on his belly and went to sleep. One of my men commented that I now had a dog.

I laughed at that and told him I never had a dog before. We had hunting dogs in the kennels at the keep and two old, retired war dogs, but none of them were pets.

"My lord, that may be, but now you have a dog."

I didn't know what to think of that. The last dog I had was when I was a kid on a farm in Ohio. The army being moved from country to country wasn't conducive to having pets.

When I retired to my tent, the dog followed me. I guess I have a dog.

Chapter 5

We received a message that a group of traders from Muscovy had arrived. We hadn't had any contact with these proto-Russians, so I was anxious to return to Owen-nap, my home and capital in Cornwall.

That was easily done as we followed the railroad tracks back to Bodmin. My men set out torpedoes on the tracks to have the train stop. These small packages of mercury nitrate would explode when the train ran over them.

They were not strong enough to cause any damage, but they were loud. Four of them in a row, a quarter mile apart, would wake up any engineer and signal them to stop. They were developed to warn of such events as bridge out ahead, but they served my purpose well.

We were waiting for it when the train stopped after slowing down for two miles. We knew its normal speed and could guess where it would stop. My people were so confident that they started a betting pool. Each person in the pool drove a stake near the tracks where they thought the train would stop. No stake could be within ten yards of another. Forty stakes covered four hundred yards.

They were very confident about where the train would stop. From the locations, you could tell they thought the engineer would hit the brakes at the first sound.

From my misspent youth in Ohio, I knew the engineer would wait until the second small explosion before taking action. Not that I ever put torpedoes on the tracks! Well, never more than one. We wanted to wake the engineer up, not stop the train.

Because of this ill-gotten knowledge, I put my stake four hundred yards further down the track. Sheer luck had the boogie wheels of the engine across from my stake.

While we had been gathering our gear to depart our camp, I had a shadow. My new pet dog was on my heels constantly. He knew who was feeding him!

At first, while he wanted to be near me, he was shy about me touching him. When we got ready to move, that changed. Clinging would be a good word.

When it was time to board the stopped train, the dog let me pick him up and carry him aboard the one-passenger car. Most of my troops had to ride on flat cars that had goods on them.

Now, I was faced with the decision of letting the train go forward to the silver mine or start backing up to Bodmin. I decided to back up. I wanted to get to Owen-nap as soon as possible.

There were only a dozen passengers in my car. After apologizing, I found out that no apology was needed. These were mine workers returning after a three-day leave. They were all tired and hung over. Since they were all scheduled to work immediately after arriving, they welcomed the additional time to recover.

I had been ready to give them silver in compensation for the delay. Now, it seemed they should be paying me.

Dog and I settled in for the trip to Bodmin. He sat at my feet. More accurately, he sat on my feet. He wasn't going to let me get away.

The trip to Bodmin was only four hours. It would have taken us two more days on horseback. I had left a party of ten to bring the horses back to Owen-nap.

The train didn't have room for the horses or facilities to load them. They would be taken to Bodmin, where they would be loaded on one of the box cars labeled 40 and 8. I whimsically had all our box cars labeled that way. The French had that stenciled on all their box cars in World War I. It stood for forty men or eight horses.

After the war, veterans formed 40 and 8 social lodges in remembrance of their crowded trips. 38 and 8 would have been more accurate, but the French must have thought that wasn't poetic enough. It was a shame the French language would never develop due to my changes. They may have been snooty about it, but it flowed off the tongue. That is, if you could pronounce it correctly.

My father-in-law in uptime was a Marine with the Marine Brigade of the 2nd Infantry Division in France in WWI and belonged to the 40&8 group in our hometown. They had a mockup of a boxcar that they used as a parade float. He suggested it might have been a good idea to have a few of those 40 *hommes* clean up after those 8 *chevaux* before his outfit boarded.

I couldn't. I made many a Frenchman wince at my attempts.

Changing trains at Bodmin, we proceeded to Owen-nap while a much-recovered group of silver miners were left on board the train for their journey back to the silver mine. A fresh train crew took over the engine and was working up steam as we boarded my special train waiting for me in Bodmin. I had radioed ahead and ordered it to meet me in Bodmin.

The silver miners thought they would get another evening of leave in Bodmin, but I knew that wouldn't end well, so I arranged for them to start their journey back to the mines immediately. I probably lost much of the goodwill that had been generated by the extra delay in their return to camp, but so be it.

It was a tired, stinky crew that arrived in Owen-nap. And my dog went straight to the kennels. The kennel master hadn't retired for the night, so I instructed him to clean up the pup and bring him to me the next morning. The pup was a mess; his fur was matted and thick with nettles, and I knew he had fleas because he generously shared them with me. There was probably a tick or two in the mix.

I needed a name for the pup. Also, I couldn't keep calling him a pup. It wouldn't be that long before he would be taller than me when he put his paws on my shoulders.

The kennel master and I talked about a program to house-train him. I knew what Eleanor would have to say about dog poop in our living quarters. When he was full-grown, it would be a big pile of poop!

One of the kennel boys would take him out after every mile and every hour in between. He would be exercised near the kennel so he could meet other dogs to socialize him and give him a lot of smells he could mark over.

I took a shower and crawled into bed with a sleepy Eleanor. We kissed briefly and then went right to sleep.

In the morning, I woke up to two children climbing all over me. They were glad I was home. Their mom sent them downstairs to pester the cook into giving them an early breakfast. Most likely sweet rolls and juice.

Eleanor and I performed our morning rituals and joined the kids for breakfast. As I predicted, the kids had sweets but were still hungry. I was always amazed at how much they could eat, but then they ran all day long.

While working on my second cup of coffee, I saw the kennel master across the room. I gave him a hand motion, and he either had read my mind or decided on his own what action to take.

A grey lightning bolt rushed across the room and jumped onto my lap. I almost spilled my coffee.

Pup was licking my face. The kids were taken aback at first, then wanted to pet him. He allowed it, which surprised me until I realized that our "pack" had a smell that made them acceptable to him.

The dog had been cleaned, and his coat brushed until it shined. He still was scraggly looking with his ribs showing.

The kids oohed and aahed over him. Even Eleanor was welcoming as he licked her face.

Cathy asked, "What's his name, Dad?"

"I haven't named him yet."

"Where did you get him?"

I went on to tell the story of his arrival and adoption.

Doug said, "We should call him Journey."

"Why Journey?" I asked.

"It sounds cool, and the name seems to fit him."

"Journey is it then."

The newly named Journey didn't seem impressed as he put his paws on our table and licked the plates clean. He was going to be a big one.

I explained to Eleanor and the kids that I had arranged with the kennel master to housebreak him.

The kids weren't that impressed, but Eleanor told me my plan was good. Otherwise, I would spend my days cleaning up huge mounds of poop.

It was interesting that not once was it suggested that Journey be relegated to the kennels with the hunting dogs. Journey was a member of our family from the get-go.

I changed the subject with Eleanor.

"What about these traders from Muscovy?"

"They arrived late two days ago. They came on a ship from Jutland. They came in a caravan from Muscovy to come here."

"Who has been talking with them?"

"John Chandler has a man who speaks their language, so he has been hired as our interpreter."

"What did they bring to trade?"

"Furs," she told me.

That answer stopped me for a moment. In my time, the trade in furs had reached a standstill in America and most of Europe due to animal rights activists. Any woman bold enough to wear a real fur coat would soon have it damaged beyond repair by a bucket of paint.

Why these thugs were never jailed was strange, but it was how it was. They paid a small fine for destroying a five-thousand-dollar garment and were free to do it again.

Here and now, that wouldn't be a consideration. I had never seen a woman wearing a fur coat in Cornwall, but I knew that was about to change.

I asked, "Are they still in Saltash?"

"Yes, I didn't want them to see too much until you returned here."

"Okay, I will radio John and have them put on a train with samples of what they offer."

They arrived in Owen-nap soon after lunch. Radio and trains had changed a two-day trip into four or five hours.

The train trip and the sights along the way left them subdued. I don't know what they were expecting, but it wasn't steam tractors plowing huge swathes of land in one go or factories belching smoke.

That reminded me I had to install filtering systems to collect the fly ash. I remembered what Sparrow's Point in Maryland looked like when Bethlehem Steel was working full blast. The tree leaves were red and dying.

I was going to prevent that early on. The fix was easy and didn't cost that much in the scheme of things. I dictated a quick note to one of my aides and turned my attention to the new arrivals.

The interpreter, Thomas Saltash, introduced the merchants. They all had the title of Boyar, which told me they were minor nobility. That or they had promoted themselves. It didn't matter to me.

We went through the normal question-and-answer period. I questioned, and they answered. From there, I asked for samples of what they had brought in trade.

They had fur from foxes, sables, minks, wolves, rabbits, lynx, and wolverines.

I told them we had many red foxes, rabbits, and occasional wolves. Artic fox furs would sell well. Lynx and wolverines would be in demand for distinctive patterns. Mink and sables would be in high demand for their natural beauty.

Then I asked what they wanted in return. They weren't completely sure. They didn't know what we produced. All they knew was that we were reputed to make many magical things and were fabulously wealthy.

I guess we were rich by their standards, and as had been said in my time, anything advanced enough would appear to be magic.

Chapter 6

Since the Muscovites didn't know what we produced, I arranged a tour for them the next morning. It would include everything but weapons manufacturing. We wouldn't hide the weapons from them, but we would not show how they were made.

They were shocked after seeing everything that could be covered in one day. We had wealth beyond their wildest dreams, at least in their worldview, which is why even our lowest serfs lived better than most of their nobles.

I tried to explain that we didn't have serfs. Our people weren't bound to the land. The farmers who worked the land could move about to other areas if desired. Of course, if they had an agreement for many years, they had to honor it.

They were amazed when I told them I was selling the land to the farmers. They couldn't comprehend that a farmer owning the land made him work harder and produce more, yielding more tax revenue.

I finally gave up trying to explain our way of life.

I ended with, "All I can say is look around you. It is working for us."

That was at dinner. The next morning, trading got serious. The Rus wanted mirrors and telescopes. These were small items that had high value.

We didn't have anyone who dealt directly with furs. If our people wanted rabbit fur, they went out and hunted rabbits. I finally had a tanner and seamstress brought in to find mutual value.

I knew that sable and mink were costly in my day. They hadn't been hunted to near extinction here, so they would be worth a little less. The question was how much less.

As I thought of them, the Russians solved the problem for us. They wanted the mirrors and telescopes so badly that they offered two furs per item. According to my two experts, making a coat would take 50 to 60 furs. That would make a mink coat sell for about four thousand silver.

That was expensive but in line with the pricing from uptime that I was aware of.

To test the waters, I had my people ask for four per mirror or telescope. We ended up at three furs per item.

The Russians had brought ten thousand furs to buy a combination of 3300 mirrors or telescopes.

This cargo fit their wagons nicely, so they were delighted with the exchange. From their conversations, they expected to make ten times the value of the fur they had brought. They would be rich if they could reach Muscovy alive.

Eleanor came up with a good idea. We could send them back on one of our schooners, plus provide an armed escort to Kyiv. The escort would have radios with them to keep in contact with us. The idea was to set up a diplomatic mission with the Khagan who headed the Khaganate. I guess they referred to themselves as Rus', where Russia came from. They were ethnically Varangians, a subset of the East Slavs.

That was from my textbooks. They were a new formation and not a country yet. They didn't even have a written language as what they spoke rapidly departed from the south or Polish areas they were migrating from.

The escort I was sending was one hundred men strong. They had orders to set up a headquarters in or near Kyiv and open relations with the Rus'. Follow-up groups would include construction workers building a keep that the Rus' couldn't take. With this new country forming, several leaders would try to be the local strong man.

It would be a long-term project, but I hoped to conquer the Rus' from within. The Mongols would be knocking on our door soon enough. A strong border here would help. If nothing else, it would direct the Mongols south to Poland, where there would be easier conquest.

Cynical and cruel, maybe, but the Mongolian Hordes were nothing to take lightly. No matter what our weapons were, there were so many of them they could overrun us.

I looked at this as a long-term investment, but who knew?

While thinking about world domination, I had some nicer thoughts closer to home. Before I instituted better health care, the death rates due to accidents and disease were much higher. This death rate left many orphans.

There were so many that they couldn't be absorbed into their relatives if they had any relatives. A crude orphanage system was in place but was only a mild step above a sweatshop. The kids were worked day and night with poor nutrition. It wasn't a death sentence to be committed to an orphanage, but close to it.

I changed that as my power spread. Now, the kids didn't work outside of the orphanage. They raised gardens, did the laundry, and kept the place clean. They received health care and education.

One thing they were lacking was toys and sports equipment. I provided them directly. These toys included everything from baseball equipment to jump ropes, jacks, Cornwall logs (Lincoln logs in my time), and doll babies.

In short everything I could think of that a kid would like to play with.

I couldn't go to every orphanage in person and hand the toys out, but I did select several new ones every year to visit.

One I had never been to before because it was out of the way was near Brude. I had business in Brude earlier in the day, so I stopped at the orphanage on the way back to Owen-nap.

It wasn't meant to be a surprise visit, so I had word sent in advance that I would be there this afternoon.

When I arrived, all the children were lined up outside to welcome me.

Two little girls came up to present me with some flowers. They were cute as kittens and were dressed in brand-new dresses. They looked as though they had never been worn before.

Looking at the line of fifty children, I realized they were all in new clothes. These must have been pulled out of storage in honor of my visit.

The matron of the orphanage was there front and center. She welcomed me effusively. Standing beside one of the young ladies, she reached to put her arm around the girl. The girl flinched as though a snake was about to wrap around her.

I was looking at the matron and saw the look that crossed her face when the girl pulled away. It was the most hateful look I had seen short of battle.

There was something not right about this. I didn't react but returned the matron's greetings as though nothing was amiss.

Smiling, I asked her if I could tour her orphanage. She looked as though she had bit a lemon but said yes.

Her "yes" may have been encouraged by the fifty troops that were my escort on this trip.

She took me through the boys' and girls' dormitory rooms. They were neat and clean. I did notice that the beds had a very thin blanket for this time of year. Especially since there was no coal in the coal scuttle to fuel the Franklin stove.

I asked the matron if I could eat with the children since it was near lunchtime. At her look of panic, I told her my soldiers had their food and would fix it themselves.

She hesitated but said yes, then asked to be excused as she had to talk to the cook. She left me alone in the barracks. I took the opportunity to look through the closets to see what the children normally wore.

It was hard to call what was hanging there clothes, rags more like it. One thing about the children still lined up outside was that none wore shoes. I couldn't find any in the closets.

Something was definitely off about this orphanage. I heard the matron returning and managed to return to where she had left me. I stood there as though I had been there all along.

We moved to the large dining room, where all the children were being led in by one of her assistants. Her assistants looked like they should have worked as bouncers at some dive bar on the docks.

The children quietly filed in. They were uncharacteristically quiet for such a large crowd. One hundred children should make more noise than I was hearing. There was no more than a murmur from the whole bunch.

Now that I was closer to them, I realized they looked malnourished. Someone would pay for this.

The matron wanted me to sit at a head table with her, but I insisted on sitting at a table with some young teenage boys.

You could see the terror in their eyes when I asked if I could join them. They all sat straight at the table, staring straight ahead.

I sighed and said, "It's a hard-knock life."

The boys looked at me out of the side of their eyes but kept their heads pointed forward.

I was sitting with my back to the matron so she couldn't see me as I quietly asked, "Is it as bad here as it looks?"

One of the boys whispered, "It's probably worse. She hires the boys out as laborers at the coal mine. The girls are sent to service in the baron's house and other rich people."

"How old are you before you are sent out?"

"To work, every one of us."

There were children here as young as four years old.

I stood up and gave a sharp blast on the whistle I always had on me. Ten of my troops came running into the room. The others I knew were surrounding the buildings. They didn't know what was happening, but my signal told them of trouble.

"Sergeant, arrest all the adults."

"Yes, sir."

At that, the matron and her thugs were taken into custody. Searching the rest of the building found a cook, two assistants, and an accountant in the offices.

Our prisoners were searched and handcuffed. The two thugs had brass knuckles on them. These weren't items needed to control small children.

The matron was stoic and wouldn't respond to any of my questions. Using standard police tactics, I questioned the adults separately. The thugs were exactly that and stupid to boot. They readily admitted to taking the children out to work each morning.

The only reason that they were here today was that it was known that I visited orphanages on my trips, and the matron didn't want to be caught out.

The cooks knew what was going on and took it all passively.

The accountant was a different story. He tried to bargain his way free when he was brought to me.

"I will tell you all if you set me free."

"That's not going to happen."

"Then I have nothing to say."

"Your books will speak for you."

At that, I opened one of the ledgers on his desk.

"Baron Brude paid ten silvers for two serving girls last week."

From there, I read off a list of monies collected for illegal child labor. I was sickened when I got to the boys sent to the mines. Several names were crossed off with the notation, "Died in mine. Five silver penalty."

One thing I could say about the accountant is that he kept meticulous books. He wrote down the names of everyone involved.

There was a safe in his office which contained about fifty gold. That didn't seem very much for all the labor being hired out.

When I asked the accountant, he got a shifty look.

"If I tell you where the money goes, will you free me?"

"You don't understand. The only choice you have is a quick or slow death. That's up to you."

He was close to crying when he told me, "It all goes to the orphanage board of directors."

"Quick it will be."

At that, I pulled out a pistol and shot him twice, once in the heart and once in his head.

I told his corpse, 'I'm a man of my word."

Using the portable radio, I ordered a full brigade of five hundred troops to get here as fast as possible.

Chapter 7

By the time the troops I had ordered arrived, we had compiled a list of names of everyone involved. That included those who were profiting from child slave labor to those using it. There were seventy-seven names on the list.

When the troops arrived, they were dispersed to arrest everyone on the list. The prisoners were taken to Baron Brude's Keep. Even the baron was involved, so he was arrested.

Not all involved were equally guilty in my eyes. Those profiting were the ones deserving the most severe punishment. I had the eleven profiteers hanged two days after the arrests. Those hanged included the matron, the baron, and the nine members of the board of directors of the orphanage.

I was left with sixty people to punish in a lesser fashion. I decided to send them to a station on the Niger River where we had the recent deaths. Replacement personnel were needed, and we had few volunteers for some reason.

There were far more than the prisoners involved. They all had families who had benefited from the orphan's work. Anyone in the family over eighteen years of age was automatically sent with their parent to the settlement. Those aged fourteen to seventeen were given a choice.

Accompany the parent or join a willing relative. If the child had no parent or relative, they would be sent to an orphanage. Not the local one.

Any child thirteen or under would go to a guardian or a distant orphanage.

Baroness Agnes and her staff arrived with soldiers. They took over the orphanage and saw to the health and nutrition of the children until a new staff could be recruited.

I created and funded a new department under Baroness Agnes's command. It was the Department of Orphans. Its personnel would perform random audits of all orphanages and operate a training school for new orphanage directors and major staff. This sad state of affairs wouldn't occur again on my watch.

§ § § §

Unbeknownst to me, a young man named Bartholomew Owen-nap was making some interesting discoveries at the time. As he was known to his friends and classmates, Bart was a sophomore at the recently formed engineering school. Sophomores were the first class going through the three-year program. He would be a senior next year. We would skip using juniors.

The tall, thin young man was interested in the properties of petroleum oil. Its many variations intrigued him. Today, he was experimenting with a new distillation called gasoline.

He knew it was a volatile substance but not how volatile. He had an open one-gallon can of gasoline. Bart approached the open container with a lantern in hand. It was late evening, and the lighting was poor.

When he went to set the lantern down next to the container, the fumes in the air ignited. The can gave a whump sound as its sides pushed out from the sudden ignition of its contents.

Bart was lucky. He only lost his mustache and eyebrows, along with his bangs. His face was red from a mild burn. He rubbed his mustache in thought. The mustache fell off in white hairs which had burnt.

He was concentrated in thought while he rubbed the ashes of his former black eyebrows. The sides of the container had bulged out when the gasoline ignited.

Could gasoline be burnt and create enough pressure to move a cylinder like steam? A liquid fuel would be more convenient than having to shovel coal. He had to get permission to perform some experiments.

About the lost hair from the sudden ignition, he shrugged his shoulders. There was no girlfriend in his life to care about it.

§§§§

Baroness Agnes reported back to me on her team's survey of all the orphanages. No others were involved in illegal child labor. The children were involved in legal labor, such as maintaining their home farm for fresh food. Other endeavors were doing their laundry and doing the housekeeping chores. These were all encouraged and well within the children's capabilities.

One enterprising group had a large open forest next to the home, so they collected downed wood and made charcoal, which they sold at a local market. These kids were the best dressed, well-fed, and had the best average grades for their class level.

They were doing well enough that those involved had bank accounts. They could have been alone if they weren't so young.

I inquired how this came about. One of the staff made charcoal in his youth. Now that he was retired and working at the orphanage gratis, he regaled the children with tales of his youth. Several clever ones talked him into showing them how to make charcoal.

Since the mudded dome couldn't be left alone at any time, as it could burn through and destroy the wood, they had to recruit others to help them man the around-the-clock shifts.

Agnes reported they were now looking at a small sawmill as there wasn't a local source of planks or two-by-fours. A side note: I had decreed that a two-by-four would be exactly that, two inches by four inches. I wasn't going to allow the shrinkage creep of board size that was prevalent in my time.

One thing Baroness Agnes found was a problem with the charcoal operation. There was no accounting. There were no signs of dishonesty, but it had to be cut off at the pass. They had an accountant set up the books at the orphanage and train four children how to keep the books. These books would be included in the annual audit of the orphanage.

The children's decision to select their work and make money was so successful we wanted to spread it to other orphanages. Several better-spoken boys were chosen to go to other orphanages and share what they had done. They went in teams of two with a prepared presentation. If they had a projector, it would have been a PowerPoint.

An adult accompanied each team. Teenage boys could get up to no end of mischief if left alone. It was a sad statement that we couldn't let any of the girls out on this duty as they would be in danger and not receive respect when they gave the presentation. It was still a backward world in many respects.

Chapter 8

As the orphanage teams made their presentations, they also investigated what natural resources were available for the local orphanage to work with. Twenty percent of the orphanages didn't have anything available, or if it was, it would be in direct competition with local workers.

I paid for the young children to clean the sides of the roads. Litterbugs weren't a modern invention. I even introduced the signs saying, "This stretch of the road kept clean by (fill in the blank business)." I about choked when I saw a sign giving credit to Madam Helen's Whorehouse. I bet the days when the ladies picked up the trash, the road was well-traveled.

I was disappointed later to find out Madam Helen hired workers to pick up beside the road. It seemed that some transactions were off the books when she had the ladies doing it.

The trash removal program became such a popular advertising method that the orphanages were crowded out of business.

I finally decided that I was spending too much time on this and turned it over to Baroness Agnes to sort it out. That may have been a mistake because she decided that no child should have to work. Instead, she instituted an allowance for each child. Paid for by yours truly.

If any children wanted to keep making charcoal or any other money-making schemes, it was on them. The orphanage's only involvement was keeping track of payments and auditing the books.

§ § § §

Bart Owen-nap was nervous as he got ready to ignite, hopefully, the vaporized gasoline mixture he had just injected into his roughly built piston and cylinder arrangement.

The vaporized gasoline was the result of trial and error. Bart had tried to ignite liquid gasoline. This method resulted in a quick gasoline burn with no explosive force. That was until his third try when he approached the liquid sitting in his warm workshop.

He wanted to get it done with as the fumes were getting stronger. He didn't lose his eyebrows this time, as they hadn't grown back from his original accident.

The fumes flashed with even more vigor than the first time. It was a wonder Bart wasn't severely injured. The stout leather apron he wore protected his body from the worst of the flash.

His head was slightly turned so his eyes didn't take the full brunt of the force. He did look slightly toasted.

That was when Bart realized that when the fumes ignited, they released more energy than liquid gasoline.

Previously, he had rescued a failed attempt at a steam engine model. The cylinder and accompanying piston were fit for his test, but the rest of the engine didn't meet the blueprints submitted, so the teacher had failed the model.

The disappointed student then junked the model and started over. Bart asked for and was permitted to rescue the rig.

All he needed was to test the power of ignited gasoline fumes to see if they could move the piston inside the cylinder. He did not want another burned face, so he put a bare electric cord through the steam injection port.

He had enough room to squeeze a rubber bulb of liquid gasoline into the same port. Experimenting had shown when he did this quickly with a small amount of liquid, it would vaporize.

He hoped that igniting gasoline vapors inside the cylinder would burn off with enough power to move the piston. For this attempt, he was well back from the cylinder when he sent a jolt of electricity down the wire to create a spark to ignite the fumes.

Nothing happened.

An instructor nearby asked why he was swearing. When Bart explained his most recent failure, the instructor explained that he had set it up wrong. The electricity had nowhere to go. He needed to have a piece of metal near the end of the wire so its current would jump the gap and create a spark, igniting the fumes.

Finding the correct distance between the wire and the metal took ten tries, but he finally got an impressive spark to jump the gap.

Due to his commitments as a student teacher to pay for his advanced schooling, it was another two days before his next attempt. During the two days, he learned he had a new nickname from the young people in his classes. It was "Old Burnt Face."

This nickname was said with laughter mixed with contempt. One attractive young lady defended him by saying that his good-looking features were now even more handsome as he looked rugged.

She was only two years younger than him, and if it weren't for school policy, he would have asked her on a date.

That is if he wasn't so shy around women.

All Bart was thinking at his next attempt on his modified setup was, *I hope this works.*

He threw the switch on the electrical generator to send a current down the line to create a spark to ignite the fumes. This time, he got a result.

Not the one he was looking for. He had removed the cylinder and piston from the failed model. In doing so, he unbolted the cylinder from the metal plate supporting the cylinder.

He had set the cylinder on the workbench without thinking of fastening it down.

When the fumes ignited, the cylinder "bucked" and rolled off the workbench. Energy had been released, but Bart couldn't tell if the piston had been moved.

After another two days between attempts and answering the questions, the cute young lady stayed after class to ask him if he had the device bolted down. Somehow, the young lady had invited herself to this trial.

She had to because the clueless Bart didn't interpret the signals she kept sending.

After thinking about his failure to get a reading on his last test, Bart bolted the cylinder to a base and rigged up a calibrated lever requiring five-foot pounds to move it. It was attached to the end of the piston rod.

Elizabeth told him this was quite clever of him. He smiled and managed to get out a strangled thank you. He would rather get burnt again than talk to any young lady. Especially Elizabeth. She was the nicest, prettiest girl he had ever met.

Now he wanted success more than ever. He had to show this beautiful young woman he was worth her time.

With that thought in mind, he cranked the electrical generator. With a thunk, the piston pushed the lever back, showing that at least five pounds of torque had been achieved. He was so amazed that he reflexively hugged Elizabeth back when she hugged him.

He would never know how this turned into a kiss, but he was smart enough to go for a second round.

The next week was exciting for both the young people. They were amid young love and had an exciting project to work on.

Elizabeth proved to be an able partner in the project. They had to design, conduct, and record experiments to optimize the use of gasoline as a fuel.

They knew that they could create at least five-foot pounds of torque. Now, they needed to know what they could achieve under current conditions. It proved to be six and a half foot-pounds. They replicated this with a dozen trials to prove it wasn't a fluke.

Next, they varied the amount of gasoline injected into the cylinder. They were able to establish three thresholds. The first was when there wasn't enough fuel being combusted to move the piston. The third is too much fuel flooding the piston and not burning off.

It also turned out that if there were too much air in relation to the amount of fuel – too "lean" a mixture – or too much fuel in relation to the amount of air – too "rich" a mixture, the spark wouldn't ignite anything at all, so part of the experiment turned out to be devising a way to get the mixture right. Later, they would learn about carburetors.

The sweet spot was achieved by varying the gasoline injected until the maximum foot-pounds were achieved. They were just a shade under seven foot-pounds. Running the same test multiple times, they were able to prove this was reproducible.

All of these experimental runs were recorded in a notebook.

Bart was about to call it a victory and move on, but Elizabeth came up with one more variation.

"Bart, what about the weight of the piston being moved and the friction required to start movement and continue it."

"You are right! The lighter the piston and the less friction, the more force can be generated. That's why I love you. You are brilliant and beautiful."

Bart had lost his shyness around girls, at least Elizabeth.

They weren't able to proceed quickly on this next step. They drew up designs of different size pistons. They soon realized the constraints they were working under. Only steel would stand up to the repeated ignition and back and forth of the piston.

This need for steel made the weight constant unless they changed the piston's diameter or stroke.

They drew up a designed experiment of the different variations using a nested design to reduce the number of test pistons that would have to be made.

These experiments wouldn't be a cheap endeavor, so Bart and Elizabeth wrote a paper based on their experiments to optimize the foot pounds needed.

They were almost ready to turn it in when they had an oops moment. They could move the piston in one direction, but how would they get it to retract?

They came up with a two-cylinder crankshaft. When one of the pistons was being ignited and pushing out it was also pulling the second piston back into firing position. It also transformed continuous rotary motion into a linear reciprocating motion.

They made up drawings of what they were proposing. The piston, cylinder, and crankshaft combination they wanted funding for would cost a small fortune to build. The tolerances involved in the fit between the piston and cylinder dictated it would be a hand-crafted device.

If the concept proved to work, someone would have to figure out how to mass-produce the parts.

They wrote their proposal, submitted it to the school's project review board, crossed their fingers, and waited.

§ § § §

Entering my office, an aide was waiting for me. An aide was an unusual event. I raised an eyebrow and summoned him forward. I assumed he wanted to hand me the folder he was carrying.

It was a thick engineering notebook with two cover letters.

I read the top one first as the aide refilled my coffee mug. It was from the engineering school's project review board. It briefly stated that this project appeared to be one I wanted to be made aware of as soon as possible.

The second cover letter described the contents of the notebook. It stated that the project notes were on developing an internal combustion engine fueled by gasoline. They were requesting funds to build a prototype based on their findings.

It was submitted by Bartholomew Owen-Nap and a lady named Elizabeth Farmer. Both were at the engineering college; he was a recent graduate, teaching to pay for his advanced degree, and she was a student in his classes.

A quick review of their notes told me they were on the right track to produce a true gasoline-powered combustion engine. This invention was big!

Setting down the hot mug of coffee that had just been handed to me, I told the guards outside my office to form an escort party to accompany me to the Owen-Nap Engineering College.

The guards had a system set up where they pushed a button next to their guard station. This button set off an electric buzzer in the nearby guard barracks, where a team was always on standby for my movements.

There had been enough attempts on my life that no one questioned the expense. At least not publicly.

Chapter 9

Arriving at the school, I went to the dean's office. There were enough labs I couldn't randomly search for the two young scientists.

Dean Tanner held out his hand to his male secretary. It seems they had a bet on when I would arrive. The dean had bet on sooner rather than later. The secretary thought it would be after lunch.

"They are in Lab 301, My Lord. I will show you the way."

We formed a column to fit in the narrow halls of the school. From the number of footsteps behind me, we were picking up people as we went.

The dean opened the closed door of Lab 301 to find the young couple in an impassioned embrace, kissing.

The dean was sputtering something about school policy while I said loudly, "Get a room."

The young lady replied as she disengaged, "I thought we had."

I had to laugh at that while Dean Tanner had enough wit to quit talking.

I went right at it, "Show me what you have."

They had been thinking ahead of the possible reaction to their announcement and had their most recent experiment set up to run.

The young man, who I assumed was Bartholomew, told us that this setup would generate seven foot-pounds of power. He showed us the certificate of calibration and that it matched the serial number on the foot-pound lever.

Elizabeth took over and demonstrated how they injected the gasoline into the cylinder. She showed us how she measured the fuel to ensure that she had the correct amount as listed in the notebook.

Bart, as she called him, then showed us a stand-alone device like the one that would create the spark inside the cylinder to ignite the gasoline fumes.

It was a simple setup which was pure elegance in my mind.

Liz, as Bart called her, injected the gasoline into the cylinder, and he cranked the electrical generator. You could tell when the electricity arced inside the cylinder as the piston engaged and pushed the lever forward as they had predicted.

I asked them which one had come up with the idea. They pointed at each other.

"Okay, you have left me with no choice. On your knees."

In what was becoming a tradition, I grabbed a piston shaft off the workbench and tapped their right and left shoulders.

"Arise, Sir Bartholomew Owen-nap and Dame Elizabeth Farmer."

There were gasps of surprise all around the room. We had gathered a crowd on our march to the lab. I don't know what they expected, but it wasn't this.

I know the young couple had a stunned look.

"Dean Tanner, is there a conference room that we can use? I need to talk to you and them about how this will proceed."

In the conference room away from all the hangers-on, I explained where I thought we were.

Speaking to the young couple, "You have no idea how big of an invention you have. You don't know that our world has changed."

I explained automobiles' and airplanes' impact on travel times and routes.

I told the dean that the school would get all the royalties due to them but that the project was now directly under me.

I told the young couple, "You will be team leaders for this project. The project is to build a working eight-cylinder internal combustion engine. I will be dictating reference books to give you a head start."

I continued, "This will be on the same terms as the other inventions I have supported. When you have a working model, you can start a business, which I will buy into, but you will be the main owner. I'm not exaggerating when I say you could end up as the richest people in Cornwall."

Turning to one of my ever-present aides, I told her to arrange a meeting with Thad for them. They were to be provided larger workspace and a one hundred thousand silver budget.

As an afterthought, I told the couple, "Don't forget to have tapered roller bearings between every piston on the crankshaft. The torque will want to pull the shaft in every direction as the pistons rotate in and out."

As I turned to leave, I heard, "What's a tapered roller bearing?"

Oops.

"I will dictate a book on that also. Good luck."

I returned to the keep, elated with this breakthrough by my people. I loved it when they came up with ideas on their own. As I have said many times, they were ignorant, not stupid. Education was curing the ignorance.

At the keep, I was intercepted by my son Doug. He told me it was time for us to have a bowl of ice cream. The history with him was that it was always time for ice cream. Since it sounded good, I agreed, and we went to the kitchen.

The head cook only mumbled a little about spoiled appetites as she served us vanilla ice cream with crushed strawberries whipped in.

As I ate mine, I regretted not having chocolate ice cream, but we didn't have access to South America yet.

At that thought, I stopped mid-scoop, holding my spoon in midair. Vanilla beans came from South America!

Where had these beans come from? I had a cook summoned by one of my two aides. And yes, they also had ice cream. I wasn't a Grinch, which reminded me that I had never told that tale.

When the cook arrived, I asked the source of the beans. She looked at me like I was crazy.

"From John Chandler on one of his trading ships."

Who was trading with South America? I had to find out. Hastily finishing my ice cream and getting an ice cream headache, I let Eleanor know that I was going to Saltash to talk to John Chandler and asked if she needed anything while I was there.

Of course, she wanted to know why I was running around like my hair was on fire, so I slowed down and explained it to her.

She asked me, "Why don't you radio him?"

I had been about to order my special train fired up for a quick trip. It was not fired up because it was always ready to go, but it still took a few minutes to bring the boiler to pressure.

"Oh, I hadn't thought of that."

"Well, slow down and think things through."

I went to the radio room and had a call put through to our corresponding room in Saltash. It would take time to summon John to the Saltash radio room as it was in the Saltash Keep. The radio was kept in the keep as a matter of security. There was a public radio station in midtown Saltash, but this one was for county business.

I started dictating a book on internal combustion engines as I waited. An hour and a half later, John was available.

We exchanged the usual pleasantries, and then I asked him where he got those vanilla beans. He didn't know off the top of his head, so I had him return to his expanded chandlery and search through lading lists.

The next day, he got back to me and told me they came from an Arab trader from Africa. The trader's home port was in what would be the Ivory Coast, a nasty place.

The ship's name was *Grei* or *Daring* in English. The captain and trader was Abd al-Uzza. No future port of call was listed nor were there plans to return here. Not much to go on. I sent a message to all stations for information on the ship or its captain.

I also had inquiries being made in Constantinople, as that was the most widely visited port.

Eleanor and I talked about this situation. She couldn't understand why I wanted to contact the Arab so urgently.

"James, you have built an ocean-going ship that can easily make the crossing. Why are you so concerned?"

"Love, it's not the crossing. It's about once we get there. South America has many tribes. The most powerful is the Mayan. They are at the height of their power right now. There are millions of them.

"They aren't pleasant people. They practice human sacrifice and cannibalism. I need to know where the captain of the *Grei* set ashore and who he traded with."

"Oh, that does make a difference. Do we need to trade with the Mayans?"

"They have enormous quantities of gold, silver, and gems. Besides that, there are two plants that we could use. One is the potato, a food staple as useful as wheat. The other is cocoa, the base for a delicious flavoring and a pain reliever medication.

"There are other large tribes, mostly on the Pacific Coast, namely the Moche, who are beginning to decline. They are as bad as the Mayans."

"Why are they like they are? Human sacrifices sound evil."

"These tribes are descendants of the Olmec who started the practices. Why they did it, I don't know."

"Did they continue these practices in your time?"

"No, they were destroyed by the Spanish when they came to South America."

"You may have to destroy them also. How did the Spanish destroy them if they numbered in the millions."

"Smallpox was unknown in the Americas. At first, the Spanish introduced it accidentally. When they saw how it worked, they deliberately infected entire populations. There is no way that I can do that."

She said, "I understand. That is not who you are. But at the same time, this will take a lot of thought before you send an expedition to South America."

"I want to find the Arab captain and where he went ashore."

"That makes sense now."

"There is nothing urgent about opening trade with the people of South America. We will do it in force when we know of a safe place to land and trade."

"That sounds like the best approach."

We then changed the subject to the possibilities of the internal combustion engine. I told Eleanor that if we could find a source of helium, we would have safe balloons with enormous lifting power.

When I described heavier-than-air flight, she thought I was kidding.

§§§§

Captain Abd al-Uzza of the trading ship *Grei* was sweating uncomfortably. His bound and tressed body was jostled about as he was being carried along a jungle trail.

What had started as a good trading voyage ended as a nightmare. The pox had appeared a week after the ship sailed on its trading mission. The ship made landfall four weeks later, with ninety percent of the crew dead or dying. They barely had enough hands to handle the sails. They wouldn't have made it if the weather hadn't been good and the winds fair.

By staying in his cabin when the disease was first recognized, he had delayed catching it. It was well known if you didn't come into contact with those who had developed the disease, you wouldn't catch it.

He had avoided all contact. His meals were brought to his cabin, and his bedding changed daily. One of the crew charged with the duty was flush with fever so he had him relieved of the duty. The crewman died a week later.

Their first trading trip had resulted in a potential fortune in unknown plants and a definite fortune in gold and silver at a ridiculously low price.

On the first trip, unable to speak each other's languages, they resorted to laying goods on a blanket. This time-tested method worked.

He and the other survivors managed to bring the ship to anchor near the shore. He realized that those who had made it were with him on that trip to Cornwall. They had been "vaccinated" on their arrival. He wondered if that had anything to do with them being the only ones alive.

They managed to make trip after trip to shore and lay out every blanket and hammock on the ship with trade goods. He was glad they had thrown the dead over the side without using their hammocks as was traditional.

Enough trade goods had been laid out to make him wealthy beyond belief.

Except the entire crew was seized and were being taken somewhere. At the first large town they arrived at, one crewmember was taken to a flat-topped pyramid. His living heart was cut out, and his body was thrown down to the waiting priest, who promptly started to eat the recently living flesh raw.

He now knew his fate. The captain hoped the natives would die in large numbers when they ate the crew's flesh and used the blankets and hammocks that had been in contact with the smallpox.

Chapter 10

These were good times for me. All my plans were moving forward. We weren't at open war with anyone, yet we were making inroads in all our border areas. Our culture was permeating everywhere.

When others saw our better lifestyle, they wanted it. The local rulers in the past would have tried to invade us and take it. Not anymore. We made certain they knew the strength of our weapons and the trained organization of our troops.

The odd chieftain might try to raid us, but they were put down quickly.

On the home front, things were fairly calm. I thought of the home front as two separate identities. There was Owen-nap, and then there was my family.

Owen-nap wasn't centrally located, so it wasn't logical to have it as the capital of our country. Logic didn't seem to have anything to do with it. Wherever I lived was the capital. London was the new economic center, but all considered Owen-nap the capital.

I would have to move to London and take all the administrative functions to make the change.

Eleanor and I talked about it many times and in great detail. We finally decided to make the move to tie our country together.

I commissioned new government offices in London and a new castle for us to live in. It would be where Windsor Castle stood in my time. To protect London from raiders coming up the Thames, I also had a keep built similar to the Tower of London.

This fortress was for show as much as anything. The true defense was in cannon batteries built along the Thames. With today's weapons, an invader's ship couldn't reach London. The Tower Keep was to demonstrate how strong we were.

The batteries would be out of sight, out of mind. You couldn't live in London and put the Tower out of your mind. It reminded those who lived in London who the true power was.

Owen-nap was to become a research and manufacturing center. It was already the leading city in both those areas, but it would become stronger. Saltash was its port and would continue to grow. Tintagel would become a backwater town.

Downgrading Tintagel's importance was a deliberate step as the city still harbored the relatives of King Geraint's supporters. As trade moved away from the city, their influence would wane. I had never caught them in an active plot but didn't believe for a minute that they were my supporters.

On what I considered my real home front was my family. Eleanor was flourishing. She was now involved in making the first full-length movie with a storyline.

Previous movies were of such enthralling scenes as a man walking down the street or climbing a step ladder. The most popular movie was a wedding. It played all over my country. A copy was even played in Constantinople.

Eleanor's movie had a working title, "Birth of a Nation". I tried to get her to change it without telling her why. That didn't work, so I told her the story behind the first real movie made in my time.

She told me to quit being so sensitive. We had no KKK, or for that matter, very many blacks in our population. I was the only one who knew of that movie, so if I didn't bring it up, there would be no problems.

She was correct, but it still bothered me. The original had such a negative effect on race relations in my time I had a hard time getting past it.

However, as a wise man once said, "Happy wife, happy life."

As she now asked us to call her, our daughter Catherine was growing into a sophisticated young lady. That is until she felt she had been done wrong. There was no holding the little hellcat back.

One stupid young man in her class pulled her pigtails and tried to guide her like a plow team. He got plowed.

Other than that, she was diligent in her studies. She was a dutiful daughter and paid attention when she attended meetings with me.

I didn't doubt that she was a normal thirteen-year-old and had secrets from her parents, but they were mild secrets, or her ever-present bodyguards would have discreetly informed upon her.

There was an incident of a bag of frogs being let loose in a geography class that she hated. I was certain she was the mastermind, but neither the boys who let the frogs loose nor her guards squealed on her.

I did notice that the boys ended up with extra desserts for the next month, and the guards had an ice cream party from a mysterious benefactor. I loved it. My daughter was learning how to get and keep personal loyalty through the fine art of bribery.

I told Eleanor, who replied, "Who do you think taught her that?"

On the better side, Catherine volunteered at one of Baroness Agnes's soup kitchens. No matter how prosperous we became, someone was always left behind for one reason or another.

Catherine wasn't even a front-line server unless there was a personnel shortage on any given day. She normally worked in the kitchen, helping the cooks and washing dishes.

My daughter did this for over six months before the newspaper figured it out. Then, there was a huge spread about her charity work.

The only effect was she didn't work the serving line anymore. She stayed in the backroom.

A reporter wanted to interview her. She agreed, but the reporter had to work alongside her washing dishes that day. That was her first and last interview. It seemed the reporters didn't want to get dishpan hands.

While Cathy wore latex gloves, the reporter wasn't offered any by the cooks.

Cathy still was sitting in on my meetings. She took notes and afterward asked pertinent questions. I was pleased to see that she was taking this seriously.

Well, most of it seriously; I saw one note she wrote. "Will he ever shut up?"

It wasn't about me, and I tended to agree with her.

Doug was still a carefree young man at eleven years of age. I had recently given the go-ahead for him to receive weapons training. The training was with guns, knives, and hand-to-hand.

We had a walled-in courtyard at the back of the keep for family only. Our training took place out of the public eye. The trainers were our personal guards to limit the number of people who knew Doug was being trained.

We followed the same procedure with Cathy, and it seemed to work.

The trainers had reported that Cathy was a dead shot. She seldom missed. Her banker's specials were still her weapon of choice.

Doug, on the other hand, was skilled with knives and swords. He was flexible as all get out and fast as a striking snake. It didn't take long for him to require a better trainer. He wasn't a bad shot, but compared to his sister, he was a beginner.

We had some wonderful family times in the training area as Eleanor and I also took keeping our skills fresh seriously.

It was a quarter mile around the perimeter of our courtyard, and I made a point of running five miles every day. The kids joined me religiously each morning. Eleanor was known to stay in her warm bed on cold mornings.

§ § § §

The spymaster of the Byzantine Emperor told his lead operator for Cornwall, "The emperor is getting impatient with our failures to steal the plans for their rifles and ammunition. I have held you back from using force to obtain them. I didn't want the Cornish to know the plans had been stolen. To keep our heads, do whatever you must to get a set of drawings of their rifles and bullets. A working copy of the items would be a plus."

The lead operator told the spymaster, "Getting a working rifle and its bullets will be no problem. However, the drawings are kept in a safe, secure room in the middle of their factory. It will take military action to break in and seize them."

"Do whatever you must. Just don't let it be traced back to us."

§ § § §

The Mayan King received reports that a new disease was spreading through the population like wildfire. He shrugged his shoulders when told. They had many people and wouldn't miss losing some.

He wanted this court session to end quickly. He had a headache and felt very hot. He would have a dozen slaves sacrificed to the gods so they would make him better.

§ § § §

Our finances were in good shape. The gold and silver mines were still producing at a high rate. We would mint coins once a month. We needed to keep increasing the money supply as the economy kept growing.

The United States had to go to fiat or paper money and credit to meet the money supply requirements to keep the economy going. We would be in that position someday, but I hoped not for a long time.

Knowing where the world's major precious metal finds were was a huge advantage.

As soon as we minted the coins, our local users and the bankers in Constantinople snapped them up. Their purity and milled edges were such that people hung on to them and spent the regular coinage. I doubted that other countries knew these coins existed. If so, so few were in circulation that they would disappear quickly.

We weren't at zero inflation, but I had no concerns with less than one-half of one percent.

One of the financial reports covered the balance of trade. When I first introduced the concept, my advisors were confused as to why I would care about tracking that.

Once they saw we had more money coming in from the outside than going out, they saw the light. I had to rein in their enthusiasm as they wanted to bankrupt the rest of the world if their plans went through.

I had to dictate several books on economics for them to read before they started to understand. We wanted to have trade slanted our way but not so much that a war would be started.

Adam Smith's *Wealth of Nations* hit home with them. It took a while, but it finally sank in that we wanted to have them depend on us but not to the point of jealousy.

While we were at it, I covered what trade embargoes could do. They could force a country into war like Japan in World War II or break them like Iraq.

After that meeting, I had a more serious one—not that finances weren't important, but it was a lot easier when things went your way.

My spymaster called the serious meeting. He used to have a name, but it was so little used that I had forgotten it. He was so unobtrusive that I didn't even know where he lived or if he had a family.

I knew he was on top of his job and only involved me when things were serious. Other than that, once a month, I was given a written report on the affairs of the surrounding countries and any other interesting tidbits he picked up.

This meeting started with a transcript that he had me read. It was a recent meeting of the Byzantine emperor's spymaster and his major staff.

I wasn't told, but we could also bug a room with our radio technology. My spymaster had a pickup microphone installed in the Byzantine spymaster's office!

He had a crew monitoring and writing down everything they heard from that location. To say I was impressed would be an understatement.

"You have installed bugs in the spymaster's office?"

"I'm not sure why you call the microphone a bug, but yes."

"It is hidden like a bug would be."

"Oh, that makes sense."

I had just introduced another term into this world.

"So the Emperor has given the go-ahead to break into our factory to steal our weapon plans and to kill people to get rifles and ammunition."

"I think they would even take a cannon if they could."

"What do you suggest we do?"

"We could lay a trap and capture them, kill them before they can take action, or kill the emperor."

"Killing the emperor is out. He has stabilized his empire, and that helps us grow and prosper. Traps can go wrong, so I think we should just kill the spymaster and his leaders."

"How do you want this done?"

"As soon and messily as possible. I want to send a message."

"As you wish."

Chapter 11

A disturbed Archbishop Luke came to me. It seems like the Pope was trying another power play. I read the message that Luke had received.

The Pope announced to Luke that my territories had grown so large that he sent archbishops for Ireland, Scotland, Wales, Sweden, Jutland, and two for the Frankish lands.

Luke was to remain Archbishop of Cornwall, reporting to a cardinal stationed in Paris.

The Pope told the distraught archbishop that he needed to tell me that I was expected to cede lands to support the new archbishops and cardinals.

Archbishop Luke and I were to allow this to happen under the pain of ex-communication of all my lands.

I made a few comments that had Luke telling me that I needed to go to confession this week, as while my thoughts were appropriate, the language wasn't.

How he knew the language was inappropriate, I don't know, as I was swearing in Swahili. I had picked it up in my stint in the Peace Corps.

Luke asked, "What can we do?"

"We have three choices. Go along with the Church or declare war on the Church in Rome."

"You said three things. What is the third?"

"Leave the Catholic Church."

Luke gasped, "A schism?"

"A clean break, create the Church of Cornwall with all the same ceremonies as they currently stand but disavow the Church in Rome."

You could tell Luke was upset at this thought.

"Luke, I will read you a textbook from my history. I won't dictate it to a scribe, as we don't want this information to get out."

The textbook I had in mind covered the church from its founding to the year two thousand. It was noted for being a balanced account of the good and the bad. It was denounced by both the Catholic Church and its detractors. One side for being too critical, the other for not going far enough.

Archbishop Luke and I met for two hours daily for the next week. Eleanor sat in on the sessions, but no one else. We covered there being multiple Popes at once, Papal armies and their wars, the sale of indulgences, the child abuse that the Church covered up, the vows of poverty while the Church amassed a fortune, and even the deals made with the Nazis during World War II.

Luke found the Inquisition and the suppression of knowledge among the Church's saddest chapters.

There were a lot of good works performed along the way. A distinct pattern emerged even there. The good deeds were attributed to the actions of individuals the Church later canonized. Few of these deeds were attributed to the institution.

A picture emerged of power-hungry individuals or saints working within a framework of indifference only interested in expanding their authority over people's lives. It was like every other institution created by man, except it was more successful in staying in power than most.

At the end of our sessions, Archbishop Luke announced that he was going on a retreat to ponder and pray about what to do.

It took the archbishop two weeks to reach a decision.

"James, I have prayed and prayed on this. I woke up this morning with the answer to my prayers."

"What was the answer?"

"God does not care about organizations. He cares about people. The Catholic Church cares about itself and uses people to maintain its continuity."

"What does this mean?"

"It means that we don't have to blindly follow the Church in all ways. It teaches that God is correct, but its actions towards men aren't. I'm ready to defy Rome and form our Church."

"That is a big step."

"Yes, and once taken, there will be no turning back. I have considered what we must do and what our new Church's form should be."

"Could you describe it to me?"

"The Church will have nothing to do with the secular world and its politics. We will care for the people's souls while the state, primarily you, will care for the people."

He continued, "We will not have vows of poverty for our priests or celibacy. God made man to procreate, and we shall honor that. The Church will take a vow of poverty, living off the contributions of its believers. If someone wants to leave property to the Church, it is their decision."

"I will be the first head of the Church of Cornwall and will have no title higher than archbishop. We will have bishops and several other levels, but we will never be so arrogant to build an organization where its leaders become distant from its people."

I asked, "Do you have the funding to support your priests when you change over?"

"No, but I trust God will provide."

I told him, "God has just provided. I will pay each priest's salary for the first two years."

"Why would you do that?"

"It is cheaper than going to war with Rome."

"You think Rome won't want to go to war?"

"They won't be able to afford it."

"But they have hired Swiss mercenaries to escort their archbishop and cardinal."

"The key word there is mercenaries. They work for the highest bidder. They have been known to change sides in mid-battle if paid more."

"How does that mean that Rome won't be able to afford to go to war? They will just hire more men."

I laughed at that, "What will they pay them with?"

"The money they were going to pay the Swiss with."

"My spies tell me they have already paid the Swiss. The Swiss refused to deal with Rome without advance payment."

"They will just ask for their money back."

"Luke, my friend, do you think Swiss mercenaries will give a refund?"

"I guess not. They have been paid by Rome. You will pay them again, and they will have had a successful season without having to fight."

"So you see, Luke, Rome won't be able to go to war with us."

He stuttered, "They will excommunicate us! We won't be able to baptize people, wed them, or have funerals."

"The Catholic Church won't do that, but the Church of Cornwall will be delighted to perform those and other services."

He laughed suddenly, "I will, in turn, excommunicate the Catholic Church. They won't be allowed to perform those services in our lands."

"Correct, there will be several issues that you will have to face. You will have priests who don't want to join the new Church. There will be whole congregations that will be against it. You will have to ordain replacement priests quickly."

"What about whole congregations?"

"They will have to be won over slowly. What we don't want to do is persecute any who meet with priests in secret. That will encourage resistance. We will ignore them as much as possible. In most cases, the secret services will fall apart from a lack of financial support.

"We will seize the lands and businesses that are currently owned by the Roman Catholic Church, whose congregations and priests were loyal to Rome, and use them to fund the Church of Cornwall.

"They will be funded at first by their parishioners, but it will become too much of a drain so that they will die a natural death. We will even pay any priest who wants to return to Rome."

"What about those who are militant and harm people and property?"

"They will be arrested and taken to public trial."

It took us several months to come up with a plan. Archbishop Luke used his people to plan what would take place. I lent him advisors where needed to handle logistical issues.

In the meantime, Luke wrote articles in the newspaper about abuses of the Catholic Church. He couldn't write about things that hadn't happened yet and might never do, but he still had plenty of things to ponder.

At one point, I checked into his working offices and found him with a whole scribble of scribes taking notes. He was like a swirling dervish as he dictated to one scribe and then another.

I noticed a good thing. Luke had lost weight and looked better than I had seen him in a long time.

My spies kept me abreast of the Catholic Church's new archbishops as they journeyed to their new areas of responsibility. A company of Swiss mercenaries accompanied each group.

I had each group of mercenaries approached in secret and bought them off. I would have loved to see the look on each of their archbishop's faces when they realized they didn't have an armed escort.

They all turned back except the cardinal and two archbishops going to Paris. The cardinal was made of sterner stuff.

I finally had to take him and his cohorts into custody as they approached Paris. It had taken them almost two months to travel from Rome to the Alps, cross them, and then ride to Paris. They probably could have done it faster if the cardinal rode a horse instead of in a huge wooden coach with no springs or shock absorbers.

They were placed on a train and sent via Monaco back to Italy. I even allowed his coach to be transported on a flat car. With one overnight stop, they were back in Italy in two days. That should send some sort of message. I let the leaders ride comfortably in one of my special cars to rub salt in the wound. Even their helpers were riding in normal passenger cars.

Now that the cardinal and his entourage were being sent back, things had to happen quickly.

Archbishop Luke had previously canvassed all the priests in our countries to identify those who would return to Rome or become part of the Church of Cornwall. A surprising ninety-five percent chose to switch churches.

I thought it was due to relieving the priests of their vow of poverty. Luke credited it to them learning the entire truth of the Catholic Church.

There were almost enough newly ordained priests to cover for those who left. In smaller dioceses, a priest would have to double up until help could be sent. Larger dioceses had enough deacons, wardens, and other helpers to cover all the masses.

It didn't take long for the Catholic Church to excommunicate all members of the Church of Cornwall.

The excommunication didn't have the effect they thought it would. Banns were posted, people were wed, babes were baptized, and the dead were given a mass and buried in the same holy ground as their ancestors.

Another major difference was now that our priests were being paid, they didn't have to push for funds to support themselves, only to care for the sick of the parish.

The indigent are cared for by the foundations run by Lady Agnes. This, in effect, had the Church of Cornwall asking for less money than the Catholic Church. In most cases they had the same priest performing the same rites.

Several cases occurred of priests returning to Rome who thought it was their duty to take the gold chalices used for communion and other valuable pieces. These men were chased down, and their loot returned to the church.

We published these thefts in the newspapers and the results of the ensuing trials. We sent the priests on their way to Rome. They could have the crooks. The thieves probably would thrive there. No doubt some good men thought they were doing the right thing, but since we had no way of knowing, we treated them all the same.

An unintended consequence was to trigger several hundred years early the separation of the church in Rome and Constantinople. This event further weakened the Catholic Church and the remnants of the Roman Empire. For all practical purposes, the Empire was dead.

When it came time for me to bring the small countries that made up Italy into my fold, it would make the job much easier. Especially since the break with Constantinople set off a civil war within the Catholic Church. This war set a record. They had five claimants to the Papacy at one point.

Chapter 12

"**M**ission accomplished."

That was the message I received from Constantinople. Two words that said so much and nothing. The message announced a success but nothing of the cost of the success.

The two words took minutes to decode and to get to me. The full after-action report took a full day.

The mission had been to kill the Byzantine Emperor's chief spy and his seconds before they could implement a plan to steal our weapons secrets and kill some of our citizens to obtain samples of the weapons.

Killing them seemed like a harsh reaction, but it was normal for the times and would be for many centuries to come. Some of the most brutal actions taken were in the cold war between the USSR and the USA. Both sides had been ruthless.

Our original plan had been to hide explosives in the speaker's meeting room. We had a microphone hidden there. After talking to the agent who planted it there, we realized there wasn't enough space to plant the explosives and a detonator. Then, there was the question of how to set off the detonator. It was not as if we could have someone sneak in and light a fuse.

We reviewed ways to remotely set off the explosion. When I say we reviewed, my staff reviewed and submitted a report. The report said they couldn't figure out how to set off the bomb from a distance. Not that ignition couldn't be done, but the equipment needed wouldn't fit in the available space.

Being professional staff, they also submitted a plan they thought would work.

The spymaster had his compound. There was no attempt to hide what occurred inside. It had prison cells for political enemies and contained all their espionage records.

The compound was walled on all sides, with watch towers at each corner. The walls were only twenty feet high, a weakness we could use.

The interior of the compound was lit up brightly, or as brightly as torches could make it at night. This lighting made it impossible to cross the open area of the compound without being seen. It also left the watchmen night-blind if they looked inward.

The plan was to create a disturbance at night, which would cause them to look into the courtyard. Once their night vision was impaired, ladders would be put up against two of the walls, halfway between the two watchtowers. The walls were three hundred feet long on each side.

My staff had experimented and found that with impaired night vision, the watchmen would have difficulty seeing anything further than seventy feet away. The ladders would be on opposite walls.

Two men with crossbows would climb the ladders and take a position on the five-foot-wide walls. They would kill the watchmen in the towers.

These actions went to plan on three of the towers. The single men in each tower were killed cleanly. The man in the fourth tower was not to be seen.

My commandos, after waiting for an alarm, approached the watch tower. They found the fourth watchman sound asleep. He quickly began to "sleep the sleep of the dead."

My men now had control of the entrance and exit to the compound. They now had to secure the inside. They had practiced in Cornwall with a mockup of the compound. Some servants lived inside the building, and a squad of twenty soldiers made up the guard.

The servants weren't a concern, but the guards had to be taken quickly. Our force was comprised of ten commandos and two explosive experts.

Once we had control of the top of the wall, the rest of our men climbed up. They pulled the long ladders up behind them. Because of their length, the ladders weighed over three hundred pounds each.

Hauling that much weight up had been practiced at the mockup. My men found that if they tied two ropes to the bottom rungs with two men guiding the top of the ladder, they could pull the ladder up the wall and then lower it inside to descend to the compound's interior.

With practice, they were able to do this in seconds. The operation from the ladders placed on the outside wall to be lowered on the inside took less than five minutes. The time included taking out the guards in the watchtowers.

No alarms had been raised on the outside at this time. Most citizens avoided the compound during the day because of its reputation. At night, no one would approach it. Not even thieves, as there would be no one to rob.

The main door of the spymaster's building was locked at night, as was the outer gate. A small one-man door was left unlocked at night for the changing of the guard in the watchtower.

This door was where our plan started to go awry. Our people posing as tradesmen who made deliveries had scouted the building during the day. We had won a contract to provide wine and ale to the spymaster's compound.

We took a loss on the liquids to win the contract and paid several large bribes. We thoroughly mapped the building and the location of all the guards.

Unfortunately, this was in the daytime. We didn't know a guard was stationed at the single-man door at night.

Luckily the guard was asleep, so my people could enter the small antechamber before the guard could wake up and bolt it. As our people put it, the guard reached a rope bellpull and set an alarm before being serviced.

From this point, it became a race. Our commandos had to reach the barracks where the guards' main force was sleeping before they could wake up and arm themselves for the battle to come.

Our force got to the barracks before all the guards were up and armed. Our ten men attacked the eight ready men. While they were fighting, the rest of the spymaster's guards were able to arm themselves.

Our soldiers were better trained and now were using pistols. The pistols proved to be the deciding factor. Fifteen guards were killed or wounded. We lost five men in the fight.

After the fight, the surviving guards and servants were rounded up and locked in the servant's quarters. The guards were disarmed and given bandages to use on their wounded comrades. We didn't have to help them any further.

The battle forced us to go to plan B. Using the pistols left no doubt that Cornwall had performed this mission.

We could have killed all the guards and servants, leaving their bodies in the remains of the explosion. While we wanted to leave a message that we wouldn't be spied upon, we also weren't going to be barbaric.

Our men opened the main gates to allow four wagons to be driven into the courtyard. A large crew followed the wagons. Their job was to empty the spymasters' compound of all espionage records.

A specialist team started looking for secret hiding places where more sensitive documents could be stored.

On streets further out from the compound, we had men in Constantinople city guard uniforms preventing anyone from entering this area. There was little traffic during the night, and no one challenged our fake guards.

The real guards for this area weren't known to patrol these streets. An anonymous donor contributed bottles of wine and trays of food to the local patrol house to ensure they didn't. There would be hell to pay when their officers arrived in the morning, but it was eating, drinking, and being merry tonight.

The last wagon load of documents pulled away as dawn was breaking. The specialists had found several hiding spots with additional documents and ingots of gold and silver, plus silver coins from many countries.

We stationed guards in the Byzantine's uniforms at the gate and in the watch towers. As the day crew started showing up, they were allowed into the building and taken prisoner.

We separated the spymaster and his subordinates from the other arrivals. The leaders were bound and placed in the spymaster's conference room.

The hidden microphone was removed. It probably would have been destroyed in what we were doing next, but we didn't want to take a chance on giving them a hint of how we knew what to do.

A wagon with tons of explosives was rolled into the courtyard. The commandos set the barrels of explosives in predetermined positions in the compound. The explosives would be detonated electronically from a distance. Short of a volcano, this explosion would be the biggest bang of this period.

The positioning of the explosives had been determined in Cornwall using the mockup as a model. The only difference was that we used one pound of explosives on our test. In Constantinople, it would be one hundred pounds per unit.

After all was ready, the last step was to remove all the servants, guards, and other prisoners from the compound. A team of five made a last run-through to ensure all was in place and no innocents were left behind. They did pick up a cat that had been left behind in the kitchen. The rats would have to take their chances.

Our fake guards left the compound, and all was in readiness. I wish I had been there to see the explosion. There was a heartbeat delay when the radio signal was sent. Then, the world went up in smoke and flames.

My people were two blocks away and had to run from the falling stone. Our people headed for the docks, where a schooner awaited them. The documents we had captured were already on board.

From the time of the explosion until the schooner pushed off from the dock was timed at twenty minutes.

We had left our wounded prisoners bound in an empty warehouse four blocks from the now-ruined compound.

Unbeknownst to me, the commandos had added one refinement to the operation. They had a photographer with them. Pictures were taken before the battle and afterward. They even took a picture of the spymaster and his men sitting on barrels of explosives. It was a grim series of photographs but a valuable event record.

Since we hadn't killed the guards who had been wounded with pistols, the emperor would know it was us. I had a copy of the pictures sent to him to let the reality of what we could do sink in.

Accompanying the pictures were copies of records we found when going through the spymaster's papers. There was enough information in them to bring the entire Byzantine Empire down if released.

It would take months to read and understand all the blackmail material we now possessed. An analyst team recreated Venn diagrams showing all the material we had interlocked. With this knowledge, we could push buttons to set almost any policy for Constantinople we desired.

That was the internal information the spymaster had collected. He seemed more interested in spying on his people than other nations. It made me think of J. Edgar Hoover. In fairness, Hoover's job was the internal United States while the CIA spied on the rest of the world. Well, the CIA and a host of other agencies.

The Byzantines had information about countries as far away as India. Their analysts drew up plans for war with everyone they spied on. The only one I disagreed with was what would be Afghanistan.

The Russians and the British had failed to subdue that country. I know the Pentagon had plans to take the country. I prayed that the US would never try as it would be a failure of the first magnitude. It would cost lives and treasure for naught.

Chapter 13

The Pope's silence was deafening. We had thrown his church out of our lands and formed our own, and there had been no reaction. Archbishop Luke was a nervous wreck between running all over the place, taking care of all the details required, and waiting for the other shoe to drop.

As I told him, there wasn't much the Pope could do; they didn't have the military power to take us on. Our people were talking about what was going on but taking no action, and the daily business of the church was ongoing. All we could do was wait and see.

Our spies in Constantinople reported that the eastern portion of the church was now talking about breaking away. They had been discussing this for over a hundred years, so it was nothing new. Would they finally be taking action?

If Rome was trying to get the Byzantines to join them in some action, it would explain why nothing was happening.

§ § § §

The Aztec priests were thrilled with the latest captives from the Mayans. They were members of the royal family. They had been captured while fleeing the Mayan territory.

These people would make a fine sacrifice to the Aztec gods. They appeared ill with pustules on their bodies, but it would not affect their fate. The priest wondered if the pustules would enhance their flavor.

§ § § §

Bart and his Liz stood behind a brick wall, peering through a small peephole. They were getting ready for another test on their pistons. This engine was a twelve-cylinder setup. They needed this many cylinders to make the shaft turn smoothly. Fewer made it run rough and wear the bearings out quickly, like in less than a minute.

They were anxious because the last four trials had the engine destroy itself by breaking a rod and exploding the apparatus.

The first time, they had been extremely lucky that Liz was out of the room when he fired it up and bent over to pick up a loose bolt. Since then, all tests have been run behind a safety wall. It demonstrated that they were dealing with much power if nothing else.

Holding his breath and moving away from the peephole, he pushed the ignition button.

This time, the cylinders fired up without a problem. They had managed to make what the books called a carburetor. It took raw gasoline and turned it into a vapor that could be injected into each cylinder. They needed to do a lot of work on the mixture of fuel and air, but it was working well enough for their immediate purposes.

The real breakthrough was realizing they couldn't make a complete cylinder by handcrafting. Instead, they made a cylinder housing with cylinder rings fitting inside. This change reduced the time to make one and increased the accuracy of the fit.

Besides lubricating the moving parts, they had to cool them. It would have taken them a long time to figure all this out without the books provided by Earl James.

Next, they had to make a flywheel arrangement to smooth out the power from the crankshaft. These engines were complicated. They were working with steel parts. It would require aluminum when it came time to provide engines for lighter-than-air balloons. Bart and Liz didn't even know where to find the metal.

There was a separate team looking into this. The team never had any good news to report.

§ § § §

One part of my job I enjoyed most was providing toys to schools and orphanages. These toys included jump ropes, wooden swords, jacks, and spinning tops. Simple toys that kids enjoyed.

Each year, I had them passed out on my birthday. I introduced a new toy each year. This year, it was the frisbee. We had made them by the thousands starting a few months ago. Of course, I had to flight test them in our enclosed portion of the keep.

Journey loved them and could jump into the air to retrieve one. The only part he was having a hard time understanding was that he was supposed to bring the frisbee back to me after catching it. Instead, he took them to a pile he had started by his doghouse.

He allowed me to retrieve them for reuse, but no one else. Even the children were kept away from his stash.

I had a stack when I played with him, so I didn't have to keep walking back and forth. Those that had been used before were chewed and drooled on. I considered it to be destructive testing.

I had considered having a booklet made up with all the different games that could be played with a frisbee but decided to leave it to the children to develop their games.

The gesture of passing out the toys was my way of convincing myself I wasn't turning into a monster. Many of the orders I had given would be considered murder in the uptime. Here, they were the norm. I'm not sure I was convincing myself, but I did feel good about having the toys distributed.

§ § § §

The Byzantine Emperor was in a rage.

"How dare that man kill my spies."

"Your Majesty, we don't know he had this done."

The emperor shouted, "Does anyone else have the capability to do this?"

"No other power, but it might have been done by rogue units without his knowledge."

"Do you believe that?"

"No."

"Why even bring it up?"

"By taking that as a position, we don't have to go to war with them. They would destroy our armies."

The emperor paused in his fit. After thinking for a minute, he agreed with his advisor.

"I see. This plan does give us time to find a way to get revenge for this act. Yes, let the news go out that we believe a rogue group from Cornwall did this. This news will buy us some time to plan our revenge. We can't let them get away with this. Since they killed my uncle, the spymaster, I want to kill part of his family. This action will send a message that he has gone too far."

The emperor asked, "What other damage was done besides decapitating our intelligence operations?"

"They took or destroyed all of our records. This destruction includes ways to contact agents we have suborned in other countries. The information they have could bring the empire down overnight if released."

"Maybe killing a family member is not the correct approach. It would be an act of suicide to do so."

"You show your great wisdom, your Majesty."

"Have your people devise a plan to punish them for this act. In the meantime, we will continue to play nice with them publicly."

"Command, and it will be done."

"I so command."

As the advisor left the room, he thought he might want to take an extended trip far away with all his riches. This action wouldn't end well.

§ § § §

I was getting frustrated about the lack of aluminum. The required bauxite ore was found in India, Australia, South America, southern France, and Guinea. Southern France was the closest, near the mouth of the Rhone River, but as yet outside my realm and too close to the Pope and the Byzantine Empire, while Guinea would be a coastal country in West Africa in my time. I had no idea what it was called now. Mining the bauxite in Guinea wouldn't be a problem as it would be an open pit.

The hydroelectric power required would be enormous. It would take about 15 megawatt hours to produce a metric ton of aluminum. To build the dams and turbines to create that power would be a major undertaking. Larger than anything we had ever tried. I hadn't calculated the manpower and the support structure required, but I knew we didn't have the trained manpower available. The support structure would strain even our budget.

The heck of it was that aluminum was so useful. If there were any way to do it, I would. Mining the bauxite was the easy part.

Suppose you want to turn bauxite into aluminum to make useful things. In that case, you've got to eliminate the impurities and the water and split the aluminum atoms from the oxygen atoms they're locked onto. Making aluminum is a multi-stage process.

First, you dig the bauxite from the ground, crush it up, dry it, and purify it to leave just the aluminum oxide. Then, you use an electrical technique called electrolysis to split this into aluminum and oxygen.

Electrolysis is the opposite of what happens inside a battery. In a battery, two different metal connections are inserted into a chemical compound, and a circuit is completed between them to generate electricity.

In electrolysis, you pass electricity, via two metal connections, into a chemical compound, which then gradually splits apart into its atoms. Once separated, the pure aluminum is cast into ingots, which can be worked, shaped, or used as a raw material for making aluminum alloys.

There was another, much more efficient process for refining aluminum, but the other problem was that refining the aluminum required cryolite, a mineral only found in Greenland, as a catalyst, and in addition to our not having sailed there yet, we didn't know exactly where to look in Greenland. The exact location was never specified in all the many books I had read on the metallurgical aspects of aluminum.

It wasn't complicated when you got down to get it; it just required a tremendous amount of power we couldn't provide. We couldn't do it today, but maybe now was the time to explore Guinea for a safe place to establish a port. I didn't want a repeat of Nigeria.

Once we had a port, we could look for bauxite and limestone. The bauxite is for aluminum, and the limestone is for making concrete. Next, we would check the surrounding area for a waterfall with high head pressure.

Who was I kidding? I was going to make aluminum one way or the other.

In the following days, I received reports about the cautious attitude in Constantinople. I was glad, for his sake, that he had backed off from wanting to kill one of my family.

I called a special meeting of my political advisors. It was held behind closed doors, and there was no way a spy could listen into that room. It was a room within a room with a Faraday cage between them. We didn't think other groups could bug a room yet, but we weren't taking a chance. We had a SCIF over a thousand years ahead of time.

I explained the problem. The emperor had given up on killing one of my family but still wanted to cause trouble.

Tom Smith put it well. "It sounds like he doesn't have enough to do. We should provide him something to keep him from getting up to mischief."

I asked, "Such as what, Tom?"

"I don't know off the top of my head, but those files taken from the spymaster's headquarters in Constantinople should have something."

Eleanor said, "You mean we should release some information to cause large-scale dissension in Constantinople."

"Exactly, not enough to get him overthrown, but enough to keep his attention away from us."

I added, "Good thinking, Tom, we don't want to throw them into a civil war. Now, how do we identify what should be released?"

My spymaster spoke up. I did know his name but always referred to him as "M", which said a letter that had nothing to do with his name, but for me, it was the ultimate inside joke.

"We have been reviewing the files and seeing how they are related. For example, one piece of information could bring down person A, but it would cascade to B and C, which links to many others, resulting in that civil war. We have to be careful about what we choose."

I asked, "Do you have any identified that would accomplish what we want?"

"Two files look promising, but we need to crosscheck some information. I should be able to give you an answer within the week."

"Let us reconvene here one week from today."

I didn't yield to the impulse to say, "Same Bat-time, same Bat-channel."

Chapter 14

We met the next week, and my advisors presented a plan that would tie the emperor in knots. We had evidence of his wife selling political offices. Corruption was ingrained in the Byzantine Empire, but this couldn't be ignored. She was cheating on her husband. He would have to do something to save face, but it couldn't be too severe as her family was financially propping up his rule.

The next month went by peaceably, well, calm as normal. There was a scandal in the church. One of the priests decided that if our church were separating from the Catholic church, it would be all right if he took more than one wife.

He might have gotten away with two wives, but five was going overboard, especially since he would declare a woman his wife from the pulpit. I mean that he would point at a pretty young lady and announce that, within his power, he was declaring this young lady to be his wife.

He got away with the first two, but a complaint was filed with Archbishop Luke, who didn't like this turn of events.

I don't know how it was all resolved, but I do know that the priest now sings soprano in the African choir.

I had the usual land disputes to settle and one killing to rule over. The land disputes were easy. I don't know why anyone bothers anymore. We had all of Cornish territory surveyed to a fair thee well.

The killing was more troublesome. A twelve-year-old girl had killed her father by using an andiron to beat his skull in.

She claimed he was abusing her. Examination by a nurse verified her claim. When questioned about how long it had been happening, she told the court that it had been two years.

I asked her why she waited so long and didn't seek help elsewhere.

"My mother told me I had to put up with it, or he would take it out on my younger sisters."

"Why did you decide to do it now?"

"He told me I was getting too old, and it was now my eight-year-old sister Beth's turn."

The mother verified the young lady's statement while on the stand. I asked why she didn't go for help.

"I was taught that it was the husband's right to take what he wanted. The females in the family belonged to him."

I decided that it was a justifiable homicide. The mother was sent to a convent for the rest of her life. I didn't want there to ever be a chance that she had children under her care.

The children's last name was changed to Owen-nap, and they were sent to a remote orphanage with a good reputation.

I also wrote a strong and clear editorial in our newspaper about what rights a man had over the females in his house. You can guess my position.

Since this case set a legal precedent, none of this sort reached my bench again. I did note the lower courts had nine cases of justifiable homicide in the next two months. I think my message has gotten out.

In the middle of all this, I received a sealed message. One of the three counts in Jutland had died. He had fallen from his horse during a hunt and hit his head. He lingered for two days and then died.

I immediately set in motion arrangements to attend his funeral. Count Eric had been one of the better counts. All three were good, but he was always cheerful and open to new ideas. His son Hagar was the one that Cathy had given a bloody nose several years ago.

My family accompanied me on the hurried trip. We took the train to London and boarded a fast sloop to Aarhus. Our maids had our funeral clothes packed and ready to go. They had their system for storing our clothes, so they could always bring what was needed on very short notice.

Arriving at Aarhus, we were escorted to Count Eric's Keep, or whatever they called their strongholds. It was large enough to house our entourage, which numbered ninety-some.

As soon as she saw her, Eleanor hugged Hilda, Eric's widow. Hilda looked like a wreck as her eyes were red from continuous crying.

Her children were lined up beside her. The eldest and heir, Hagar, had grown since I had last seen him. Now, he was a head taller than Cathy, and I didn't think she would be giving him a bloody nose this trip. I think I should have other concerns about how she looked at him.

We said all the right words to each other, and we were settled in our rooms. We gathered for a late meal. Later that night, we met under torchlight for the funeral. Count Eric was given a traditional Viking funeral. He was buried in a long boat with treasure and food to accompany him on his journey to the other lands.

There was a feast for the funeral guests, which lasted half the night. The other two counts were present, and we agreed to meet the next day.

I think the Vikings could teach the Irish a thing or two about throwing a wake. I paced myself, or I would have been hung over for two days.

Eleanor elbowed me at one point to get my attention. She pointed at Cathy and Hagar sitting with kids their age at a table.

You could tell they were holding hands under the table. The look on Cathy's face said that she thought he could hang the moon for her. The look on his said he would die trying.

We chuckled and let them moon at each other. After midnight, Eleanor collected a reluctant Cathy to end her evening. Cathy's face began to form a pout, but Eleanor whispered something in her ear that brought a smile to her face.

When Eleanor returned to the wake, I asked her what she had told Cathy.

"One word, 'Tomorrow.'"

"Are you encouraging them?"

"Young love needs no encouragement. We leave in two days so that the parting will be painful, sweet sorrow. But parting it will be."

I couldn't place where I had heard that saying before, but I got her point. Cathy's bodyguard, Janet Farmer, would keep her from too much trouble. I wasn't thrilled, but I guessed smooching wouldn't hurt. Anything more and Hagar would be singing with that priest in Africa. I'm her father, after all.

The next morning, I met with Counts Arne and Bjarne to discuss the state of Jutland. They had no problem agreeing that Hagar would come under my protection and the governance of Jutland would remain the same.

They were both pleased with how their country was progressing, especially because it was with little effort from them.

All they had to do was send specialists to Cornwall to learn our more modern methods and then return home to implement them.

With Jutland's increased wealth, there was less reason for their young men to go raiding. A few always wanted the adventure and what they considered easy plunder. They found out differently when they ran into one of my schooners, which patrolled the North Sea.

We agreed that Helga's brother, Aksel, would be a good mentor for Hagar. His uncle was known for having a level head and not being extravagantly involved. Everything seemed to be going well in Jutland, and the next day, we started home.

At the docks, a sad scene was enacted. Hagar and Cathy were parting for what seemed like forever. They faced each other and held both hands. They both wanted a goodbye kiss but were afraid to do it before their parents.

As I started up the ramp to the ship, I said loudly, "For god's sake, kiss her. We need to make the tide."

I didn't look back, but from the sighs of the women around me, I knew they had heard me.

Once we were home, Cathy moped around the keep for several days and then came to her normal, cheerful self. I did notice an increase in the mail back and forth from Jutland.

The bulk mail was received on a long table I passed every morning. Every morning, my daughter was loitering nearby, waiting for it to be sorted.

The mail sorters enjoyed teasing her, as hers was almost always the last handed out. One morning, she looked so distressed as they stretched things out that I commented as I walked by.

"The games have gone far enough. Hers is to be first done every day."

That got the mail sorter's attention. Cathy didn't react, but later, I got a hug for being the best dad in the world.

I wanted to develop a source of aluminum, and Guinea seemed to be the answer. A very expensive answer. That didn't mean that I couldn't start the process. The first thing that had to be done was to map the coast and hunt for a likely harbor.

This time, it wasn't to be in a low swampy area. There had to be high hills on which the settlement could be built. Before a settlement was started, the area had to be explored. That required a base camp that could grow into a city.

Once a safe camp with walls, drainage, water, and sewage was established, the explorers would start on their real mission to find a source of bauxite and a place to put a dam for hydropower.

First, I issued written orders to our new cartographic group to survey the coast of Guinea for likely harbors and safe places to build a camp. The camp would be a starting point, but depending on where bauxite was found and the nearest rivers were, the settlement might be placed elsewhere.

Another concern was the natives. We had no idea if they were a warlike or peaceful people. We could easily overpower the natives, but I would rather have good relations to hire them to work in our mines.

§ § § §

Bart and Liz were at an exciting stage of their engine development. They had finally got a cooling system for the engine that worked. The fan was so fast and blew with such power that Bart wondered if the car being built could fly. Some simple math proved that not to be the case, but it left him thinking.

The oiling system to keep the pistons and cylinders lubricated had been difficult to iron out. The breakthrough came when Liz reread one of the books that the earl had dictated. It seemed you had to filter the oil as fine metal particles would score the pistons and inside of the cylinders, causing early wear and even catastrophic failure.

They had just attached the drive shaft to the worm gear on the rear axle of their crude vehicle. If all went well, the engine would provide enough power to propel the car forward. They had read that the car could also be run backward, but that was a problem for another day.

With help, the car was pushed outside their workshop on its wooden wheels. They knew they needed inflatable rubber tires but hadn't the money to make them. They were testing if the engine would propel the car rather than the smoothness of the ride.

Their car was an odd-looking contraption. It was an engine mounted on a frame. There was no bodywork, which would come later. After Bart's catastrophic failures on the early runs, they took to heart statements made in the books the earl had dictated.

The need for a roll bar acting as a safety cage to protect the driver and passengers if there was a collision or the vehicle rolled over was self-evident. Bart and Liz knew the dangers were real if they hit something going thirty miles an hour. They had read of higher speeds in more advanced automobiles but weren't certain they accepted the claims.

Races at two hundred miles an hour weren't believable, much less land speed records of over seven hundred miles an hour. That was impossible. They could accept the necessity for safety devices at even thirty miles an hour. Reading about trains jumping the track at that speed was harrowing enough.

They installed an over-the-shoulder seat belt once the roll bar was in place. It was clumsier than the click-in device described in the books, but it worked. What they didn't have was a seat. A wooden crate of the right height was bolted to the frame.

When all was ready for the test, Bart fired up the engine with a roar. They had read about exhaust pipes and mufflers but hadn't yet gotten that far in design work.

He shifted into first gear and stepped on the gas. He didn't realize how much acceleration he would get, so he pushed it to the floor.

The car moved forward with a jerk. Suddenly, he was going ten, twenty, thirty, and forty miles an hour. The straightaway they were using wasn't very long, so he ran out of room. He plowed through a wooden fence. He got his foot off the gas and hit the brake. It was too late as he nosed into a tree at twenty miles an hour.

He found out the hard way why you wore a seat belt. The belt left him black and blue across the chest, but he was sore and alive. The car was destroyed. Bart held the record for the first automobile wreck in the world.

Once Liz established that he was okay, she was jubilant along with Bart. They had proved their engine was powerful enough to do the job!

Chapter 15

The news of Bart's simultaneous car wreck and engine success was brought to me immediately. Their research building was only a fifteen-minute horseback ride from the Owen-nap Keep. I made it in twelve.

Bart was still being examined by one of the Grey Ladies as Baroness Agne's nurses have become known.

The bruising on his chest was going to be impressive, but it appeared he didn't have any broken ribs.

"Bart, how fast did it go?"

"I don't know Earl James. It lurched when I started up and got away from me. It sped up until I managed to find the brake pedal. By then, I had gone through a fence and slowed down when I hit that tree."

"Your insurance rates will be going up."

Liz asked, "I beg your pardon, My Lord. What are insurance rates?"

"Uh, I will explain later. First, let's examine the wreck."

Bart had hit the tree square on. It's good he managed to slow down the test bed as the engine mounts hadn't sheared off. If they had, he would have been killed. The seat belt that held him in place and prevented him from flying into the tree would also have held him in place when the motor was shoved back.

As I thought of it, the front end of the test bed was shoved in. The radiator and fan were smashed, and the front frame was damaged.

Bart was in a mild state of shock, so he was escorted to our local hospital for further treatment. Dame Elizabeth and I accompanied him. By this time, a large crowd had gathered.

As we started away, I realized that I smelled raw gasoline. The small gas tank on the test bed had been ruptured. I ordered Bart's work crew to put a temporary fence around the test bed and wet the area so the gasoline wouldn't catch fire. There were no arguments as they all had seen what gasoline could do.

I remembered a scene in a movie. I couldn't think of its name, but a stunt plane had crashed, and the pilot was trapped in the aircraft. He was uninjured, but it would require work to get him out. Unfortunately, gas was spewed all over the area, and a careless smoker threw down his cigarette, igniting the area. Everyone ran away, leaving the pilot to burn alive. It was a horrid scene, but I never forgot the screams.

At the hospital, Bart was examined again, and it was confirmed that he was only bruised. He was given a strong dose of aspirin. The nurse didn't think morphine was indicated.

Once he was made comfortable in bed, I had a few questions for Bart and Liz.

"What could we have done better?"

I used "we" to show that I wasn't placing any blame on them.

Liz brought up, "Our test track was way too short. We need something at least a quarter mile long."

I had to smile at the distance because I knew where that would go.

Bart added, "The track has to be at least four cars wide, as I don't know if it was going straight."

Now, I was almost laughing.

Liz said, "We should line it with hay bales to prevent a hard crash."

I had to say, "The hay bales will prevent the cars from running into the spectator stands."

"What spectator stands?" asked Liz.

I explained that in the books, there were car races to see who could cover a quarter-mile track in the least amount of time.

They immediately understood what this meant.

Bart excitedly said, "We could charge admission to watch the races and also charge an entry fee to the racers and award a small cash prize to the winner."

Liz thought of food stands and restrooms. There would be a first aid station and even an announcer's booth to tell people what was happening.

I let the kids build on this for a while, then brought them back to the present.

"The first track will be to test the engines safely. It will be a closed track to keep this invention under wraps for as long as possible."

"We will also have to build a large oval track for testing long-distance driving and a series of road surfaces to see what the vehicle can handle."

My desire to keep things under wraps was quickly put to bed. A newspaper reporter was on the scene. He was accurate in his description of what happened. He also noted that Bart's insurance rates would increase without further explanation.

Bart was flat on his back for two days. Even after that, Bart could only walk slowly for a week. During that time, he, Liz, and I drew up plans for the tracks we would need. I had broken land that wasn't good for farming out towards Brude. It was a large enough plot to build our test center.

The whole thing would be fenced in far enough from the tracks that no one could see what was going on. Support buildings would include an engine shop, storage, a canteen, a security center, a first aid station, a fire station, and sleeping facilities.

These additions required a large increase in their budget, but I had no qualms about doing this. Our first shipment of salt, gems, and gold had arrived from Timbuktu, and "I was flush with cash".

The main research center was enlarged and fenced, and the entrance was controlled by security passes that had to be constantly displayed. Only a few of us were allowed in all areas. I even had a pass as I wanted to demonstrate I was serious about this.

Cathy whined about not having full access, but I was short with her and told her it wouldn't happen and to get over it. She didn't need to know.

She must have gone to her mom because Eleanor asked about it that evening. I told her that Cathy wanted to be able to go anywhere she wanted and that I had told her no.

"That's not quite how she told me. I agree with you. She needs to realize that there are limits, even on her."

"I'm glad you agree. Cathy wouldn't even understand what was happening in those areas and would hinder the workers."

"I put her off until I talked to you. Now I know how to respond."

"What will you say?"

"The Earl of the Marches says no, and that's it."

"Ah, so I continue to be the bad boy?"

"Yes, but I will explain why you are being the bad boy."

"Thanks, I guess."

She said, "Come here. Sometimes, a girl needs a bad boy."

The next day, we received a message from Jutland. Count Bjarne had died from a fall downstairs. This death alarmed me to no end. Count Bjarne hadn't followed the other two counts in building a keep similar to mine. He maintained the traditional longhouse. They had no stairs.

We left for Aarhus the next day. On a hunch, I had an extra one hundred troops follow on another train. Something didn't smell right in Denmark.

The steam-powered ship *Dreadnaught* waited for us in London. It was the first of its kind, screw-powered with cannons in a rotating turret. There were two turrets, one fore and the other aft. Each turret held three breech-loading, five-inch cannon. This ship was the most powerful on the high seas.

We made the crossing in one long day. That was a record and the new norm for travel on the oceans. There was enough oil in the bunkers to make another three crossings. The *Dreadnaught* is the ship I wanted for a trip to South America.

We still hadn't found any trace of the *Grei*. I still hoped to find her and her captain to find the best place to land.

At Aarhus, we were met by Count Arne. We would be staying at his keep as the late Count Bjarne's longhouse wouldn't house my party.

Count Arne looked stressed, and I asked him if anything was wrong. He asked me to wait so we could talk in private.

By the time we settled in our rooms and Count Arne and I had time for that talk, it was late evening.

"My Lord Earl of the Marches, I fear for Jutland."

"I fear the long title. Call me James in private, Earl in public."

He nodded tiredly at that.

"Now, Arne, what is the problem?"

"I think we are heading towards a civil war. Count Bjarne's death was no accident."

"I wondered how he could fall down a set of stairs in a longhouse."

"The fall was from a watchtower in his harbor."

"Oh, that makes more sense. Why do you think foul play was afoot?"

"A young man was looking through a telescope he had just received for his birthday. He saw a man hit Count Bjarne in the head from behind, then set him tumbling off the tower to the rocks fifty feet below the tower."

"Where is this young man now?"

"I have him safe in my keep. He was wise enough to say nothing to anyone and come directly to me."

"I want to speak to him later, but I have a few questions for you."

"Such as?"

"Who benefits from this crime?"

"No one that I can think of other than his heir."

"I know Count Bjarne had no children, so who is his heir?"

"That would be Alfred Neilsen, a first cousin."

"What sort of man is he?"

"Strong, dour, a strong believer in the old ways."

"Did he get along with his cousin?"

"They hated each other."

"I have learned that in crimes of this sort, you must look for means, method, and motive."

I explained, "Means refers to a person's tools or resources to commit a crime. In this case, a hired assassin or the beneficiary of the crime."

Continuing, "Method refers to how a crime was committed. Here, the count was assaulted and thrown from a great height to his death."

I ended with, "Motive refers to why a person committed a crime. Alfred Neilsen hated Count Bjarne and will profit from his death.

"If we can place Neilsen at the scene by a witness, there is a strong case against him, and we can put questions to him."

"I see. These thoughts are strong logic and make sense."

"Now, what was Neilsen's relationship with Count Eric?"

"They hunted together. They both enjoyed the outdoors and rode out for boar several times a month. Eric fell on a hunt on my land."

"Was Count Eric on a hunt with Neilsen when he fell?"

"I don't know, but I can find out easily. My head huntsman will know who was on that hunt."

"Summon him."

Count Arne sent a page who was waiting outside his study door to summon the huntsman. In less than twenty minutes, the huntsman knocked on the door. When he entered, I saw the huntsman was dressed, awake, and alert. It was late enough that it was curious.

Especially for a huntsman who would usually be up early to see the game moving around in the pre-dawn.

Count Arne asked, "Was Alfred Neilsen along on the hunt where Count Eric fell from his horse?"

"He was the one who found the count's body."

"Thank you. You may go."

"Yes, My Lord."

After the door was closed, I stated, "Means, method, motive. I'm afraid we may face a civil war if we don't act quickly. If my thoughts are correct, your life and Count Hagar's are at risk."

Count Arne wasn't a slow person, and he understood immediately.

Chapter 16

C ount Arne wanted to arrest Neilsen immediately.

"What we have is circumstantial evidence. While it points strongly by logic at Neilsen, we have nothing like an eyewitness or hard evidence like finding him at the scene of a murder with a bloody axe in his hand."

I continued, "Now is the time to talk to the young man with the telescope."

Arne replied, "I will send for Anker Pederson."

It only took fifteen minutes for the young man to appear. He was tall for his reported age, medium build with blue eyes and blonde hair. Your typical Jutlander or Viking. He appeared nervous, so I spent a few minutes asking why he had a telescope. It wasn't the normal item for a teenager in this time period.

"My uncle gave it to me when he stopped sailing. He said he no longer had a use for it, and I might find some amusement. I do like to look at the moon and stars."

"Why were you looking in the direction of the tower that night?"

"I saw a flash of light from a lantern, and it irritated me as it hurt my night vision. Nothing is ever over there in the dark, so I wondered what was going on."

I turned to Count Arne, "Do we know why Bjarne was up on that tower in the middle of the night?"

"No one seems to know."

Turning to the young man.

"I would like you to picture in your mind what you saw that evening."

"Count Bjarne had the lantern in his hand and was starting down the steps when a man rushed behind him and shoved him over the edge."

"Can you describe this man?

"That is easy. He is one of the priests who just arrived from Rome. I saw them come through the village when they arrived two months ago and see them almost daily in the town square. Everyone talked about how they never talked to the local priests or tried to reconvert people to their faith."

"You know we are no longer members of the Catholic Church but the Church of Cornwall."

"Yes, My Lord. My father is pleased we are saving two silver a week."

"So, you saw one of the Catholic priests push Count Bjarne off the wall of the watchtower."

"Yes, My Lord."

"Arne, this is why you can't convict on circumstantial evidence. We had a logical theory, but a credible eyewitness had shown it to be false.

"I have some thoughts, but before we discuss them, we need to have Anker dictate it to a scribe, and we will sign it as both hearing what is written is what he said. This becomes part of a deposition, which we can use in court. That way, we don't have to expose Anker in court."

"Where can we put Anker to keep him safe?"

"He will come to Cornwall with me. Also, Eric's widow and her son Hagar will be joining us."

Turning to Anker, "We will bring your parents here in the morning and explain to them what is happening and why."

"Good, they will wonder when they wake up and I'm not there."

"Arne, please have a messenger bring them here first and have him tell them their son is not in trouble."

I continued, "Also, have your huntsman returned for another question. Only one question."

Soon, a grumpy-looking huntsman appeared in Arne's office.

"What can I do for you, My Lords?"

"Huntsman, were any of those Catholic priests on Count Bjarne's hunt the day he fell."

"All four of them. They were a handful to keep in the hunt. They kept riding off at tangents from the hunt. It made it hard for me to keep everyone together. I was afraid that a single rider would stumble on a boar and be killed. Instead, Count Bjarne somehow fell from his horse."

"Thank you. That is the last piece of information we need from you."

"Then I will return to my bed."

The words said one thing. The tone of his voice said he didn't believe me.

It was almost midnight when Count Arne and I finished planning what to do.

The next morning, as requested, Anker Pedersen and his parents were at the keep. I explained to them that he was an eyewitness to a crime. Because of this, he was in danger. I would like to send him to Cornwall for a time. They had no problem with this. His father said he knew no good would come from giving that boy a telescope.

I didn't follow his thinking but didn't let it bother me.

While this conversation was occurring Count Arne had his guardsmen take the four Catholic priests into custody. They didn't come quietly. In the ensuing fight, three guardsmen were killed, and we were left with one wounded priest.

The guard officer reported they didn't fight like any priest he ever knew. A search of their rooms at the inn revealed nothing.

The wounded priest would live, at least long enough to hang him. When questioned, he freely told us that he was a mercenary who had been hired by a cardinal in Rome to pose as a priest and to kill as many of the heirs to the throne of Jutland as they could.

The idea was to create confusion and tension so a civil war would break out. He didn't know why that was wanted and didn't care.

I asked him to describe the cardinal. When he got to the wine-colored stain on the right side of his face, I knew it was the one I chased out of Paris.

I asked the mercenary why he was so forthcoming with the information he told me.

"That is the way the game is played. I have no animus in this. I'm only a hired man. If you don't let me go, the next time you try to hire a mercenary, you will be refused."

What he said made sense, but it depended on me hiring mercenaries. All of a sudden, I laughed.

"You are right. I would like to hire you to return to Rome and kill the cardinal who hired you."

We negotiated a price that seemed low to me, patched him up, and told him he would be accompanying us back to London, then going to Anglet by ship, then train to the Italian border. There was no Italy as such at this time. It was easier for me to think of it that way. A trip that would have taken months by land would have him there in a week. Since I had taken over all the little duchies in the area, there was no opposition to my railroad coming through.

There would be a close guard on him the entire trip.

That day, I brought Count Eric's widow, Gry, up to date on what had happened. I told her that while I thought that they should be safe now, I would prefer it if she and her children accompanied me to Cornwall. I wanted the heirs to Jutland to be spread out so it would be difficult for the cardinal if he lived long enough to try his plan again.

She hastily agreed, feeling that she and her children were still in danger. Eleanor took charge of getting her and her family ready for the trip.

Count Arne and I visited Count Neilsen. Since he had been cleared of any crime, he was now given his honors.

As I had been told, he was a dour man, but when he did smile, it was a joy to see. I told him the entire story, even the part where he was under suspicion. He laughed at this.

"It's a good thing for me that you are a thorough man. I would have hanged me for what you first knew."

"All I ask is that you remember this in the future. Get all the information before you take action."

He soberly told me he would take that to heart. I asked him if he would be staying in his longhouse or moving into the former Count's Keep.

For a second time, I got a smile, "My wife and daughters have seen the keep and its modern conveniences. We will be moving there."

§ § § §

In Rome, Cardinal Aldo was eating his breakfast while meeting with his archbishop, who was his conduit to the Swiss mercenaries.

"Stage one of my plan should be happening now. Killing the heirs to Jutland will cause enough problems to distract that damned Earl of Cornwall."

The archbishop, a pedantic man, replied, "I believe his title is Earl of the Marches."

"I don't care what title the jumped-up Kernowick uses. I want him dead, but it won't be easy."

"In the meantime, those false popes have to go. I should be the next pope."

As Aldo said this, he rubbed the wine-colored stain on his face, a lifelong habit.

"Your Eminence, I'm pleased to report as of this morning, there are only two pope claimants. Two of the others ate something that disagreed with them last night."

"I shall pray for them. Who do you think poisoned them?"

"It is rumored that Cardinals Mattia and Lorenzo ordered the killings."

"Are they going to offer themselves as pope, or are they supporting someone else?"

"Mattia and Lorenzo are cousins. Mattia is the senior and, I believe, the one to become pope."

"I will have them assassinated first."

"I'm afraid not, Your Eminence. Haven't you noticed how you are sweating and feeling ill?"

"What have you done?"

"They pay better than you."

"But you are my sister's son. How could you do this?"

"Because mother ordered me to. She has always hated you."

As the archbishop spoke, the cardinal grew weaker and fell unconscious.

The archbishop uttered, "Must have been something he ate."

§ § § §

Sir Bart and Dame Liz, as they called each other, were preparing for another trial run of their automobile testbed. This one was more sophisticated as it had a body mounted on its frame. The steel bumper on the front of the car was backed by a hydraulic cylinder to cushion any impact.

The test driver wore goggles as he would be going so fast that dust in his eyes would blind him. Bart wasn't allowed to drive anymore at the earl's orders as he was too valuable to risk.

The test driver gave all clear and pushed the starter button. They had managed to pass the hand cranking of the engine stage of automobile development. Having a cheat sheet, as the earl called the books he had dictated, helped tremendously.

The driver slowly accelerated the car, unlike Bart who pushed the pedal to the floor on his first attempt. The car picked up speed as it moved down the hay-bale-lined quarter-mile track. It never veered left or right as it smoothly accelerated.

At the finish line, the test driver slowed the vehicle down, made a huge U-turn, and trundled back. When he got to them, he had a huge grin.

"Sir Bart, I reached forty miles an hour if this speedometer is to be believed. I'm now the fastest man on earth."

"Did you press the gas pedal completely to the floor?"

"No, as ordered, I only went halfway."

"Fantastic, now I want to take a run down the track."

Liz spoke up, "Dear, you know the earl doesn't want you to risk yourself."

"I won't do anything stupid; I just want to see how it feels to drive without hitting anything."

He told the test driver, "Hold my beer. I am certain that nothing will go wrong."

Reluctantly, they allowed him to get behind the wheel. When he was buckled up, he started the engine with a mild roar.

Liz, making the sign of the cross, started praying.

Bart started out as he should, but once he was moving, pressed the accelerator to the floor, or as the earl had said, "Put the pedal to the metal."

The car reached sixty miles an hour when, all of a sudden, a dog dashed across the track in front of Bart. He instinctively turned to the left to miss the dog.

Unfortunately, he turned too quickly and put the car in a skid. The wooden wheels couldn't stand the sideways torque generated and flipped the car over, causing it to roll over several times.

When the horrified Liz and the test crew arrived, he was lying in the wreckage with a grin on his face.

"Liz, I'm now the fastest man alive at sixty-two miles per hour."

"Yes, Dear, but your insurance rates will increase again."

They both started laughing in relief.
One of the crewmen asked the other,
"What is insurance?"
"No idea."

Chapter 17

I realized later that I had made one mistake or fate had taken a hand. Our two young lovers would be reunited sooner than I had hoped. The news of Lady Helga and Count Hagar being aboard my ship had Cathy at the dock, waving like crazy.

As soon as I got back to the keep that night, I expressed my fears to Eleanor. She reminded me that Cathy was almost sixteen years old and that most young women were married at that age and had children.

This was one time that my thinking from my last life and this life was in direct conflict.

All was quiet in Jutland. Our intelligence sources report that Cardinal Aldo had died in the War of the Popes, as it was being called. I was rooting for all sides as the more they damaged themselves, the less bother they would be to me.

I had nothing against Catholics in general, but I hated the corrupt leadership.

On a better note, our relationship with the Swedes was at an all-time high. They originally allied themselves with us as they saw us as a dangerous neighbor who could overwhelm them at will. They were correct in their beliefs.

As time passed and they learned more about our standard of living, they adopted it as fast as possible. We had set up MASH units along our mutual border. They treated all comers. As the benefits of our medical knowledge became apparent, we were invited to locate MASH units within Sweden.

The area I refer to as Sweden was now known as the Norse and hadn't become a unified kingdom yet. They were working on it, but there were still many independent jarls. This was to our advantage as we could win them over one by one. In military parlance, we were defeating them in detail.

There was never a shot fired. Instead, it was a creeping culture change. When our MASH unit was set up in a village or jarl's manor, we also brought in our radios.

Their rich could buy a radio set, and we would install it for free. We also ensured that each area had radio coverage for free receivers that everyone could listen to. We would rent or build a building with seating and loudspeakers so people could come and listen to the radio programs. As things progressed, we added our movies.

Eleanor's *Birth of a Nation* had become an international favorite. It has been dubbed in many languages now. It showed the development of Cornwall.

This included everything from the wars of expansion to the invention of the flush toilet. The flush toilet and toilet paper were more talked about than the wars.

One set of village leaders approached us to see if we would help them install a sewage and water system. My people on site jumped on the request and offered them favorable terms for the construction cost. I knighted the head of that team for his quick thinking. This was what we were hoping for.

Our newspaper was now an international paper with regional inserts. One could buy or subscribe to the main paper and receive a regional insert included at no additional cost. For more than one region, the cost went up. Altogether, we now had fifteen regions. The regional inserts were printed in two sections, first the predominant local language and then Cornish.

Archbishop Luke had started the paper, but as it grew, he took it public with an IPO. He still held a majority interest, and his profits went a long way towards financing the Church of Cornwall. I was bearing the start-up cost, but he would be able to take over seamlessly.

Cornish was becoming the universal language of trade and infiltrating every region. Our Cornish wasn't the same as the original Cornish. Between my additions and all the loan words from other regions, it was becoming its own language, like English but not English.

With all these influences, the Norse wouldn't become the Swedes that I knew. They would be absorbed into our culture. Archbishop Luke used low-key proselytizing to convert them from the old religion to Christianity. Since Christianity had borrowed its holy days from several religions, it made it easier to demonstrate they were the same.

How he was able to relate Odin the All-Father to God was beyond me. God only had one son, Odin many. It was a slow, insidious process, but it appeared to work. He had set up a conference where the two religions were being compared. Commonalities were being emphasized, and differences were set aside to discuss later.

I enjoyed one argument that Jesus being crucified for Man's soul was equaled by Odin losing an eye. These guys could have been world-class lawyers. They could twist anything to their liking.

My cynicism set aside, one of the more important things we introduced was the smallpox vaccination. One clever MASH unit started using an instrument to make the scar in the shape of a jagged lightning bolt. The Norse loved it. They would come to the center and demand the mark of power, as they called it. I suppose it was a mark of power against smallpox.

I thought of a bad pun to describe how the Vikings wanted it, "Whatever floats their boat." I was smart enough not to voice it. Well, only to Eleanor. From her groan, I knew it would be a success but also could become an insult, like calling someone a hillbilly. Better left unsaid.

§ § § §

The few Aztec families left alive from the smallpox were fleeing north, taking the disease with them. The blankets they used had scabs from people who died from the pox. These scabs could transmit the disease for up to eighteen months. This is how the Europeans killed the North American Indians the first time around in the seventeenth and eighteenth centuries.

§ § § § §

Walking around the market in Owen-nap, I was amazed at the changes in the products for sale. When I first arrived, it was a true farmers market. Now, it has many other goods for sale. A few permanent stalls were in place, but no storefronts were open yet. It wouldn't be much longer before they were commonplace.

The first one was being set up as I watched. It would be a beauty parlor. They were hauling in the hair dryers now. These weren't the nice handheld ones that I knew of; these were large, clunky machines with a hose that ran to a helmet. This beauty parlor was more like those of the 1950s. We hadn't invented the transistors needed for a handheld one yet.

One stall was selling electric toasters like those of the 1920s. The toaster had a door on each side where the toast was loaded. There was no automatic cut-off or popup device. You had to watch the toast so it didn't burn. Maybe I should read up on that one. I don't think the first popup toasters were based on transistors. The popups would be less of a fire hazard.

There were washtubs and washboards for sale. These were a step above going to a stream and pounding on a rock. Next to that stall, a man was selling what looked like an early agitating washer with a mangle to squeeze the water out. It was electric-powered so it would be a huge jump in technology.

For these appliances to work, the homes had to be wired for electricity. I had an aggressive program in place to provide power to every home. The wiring would all be run underground. I didn't want to clutter up the countryside with unsightly poles and wires. The real reason was that any foreign invader wouldn't know about the wires, so they couldn't destroy the infrastructure.

The wires were run through fired clay tubing. The tubing was placed on blocks to keep it from touching the ground. Periodically, there were French drains to keep the wiring trenches from flooding. So far, they had worked, but we hadn't had a so-called hundred-year storm in a while. They weren't called that here, but folklore talked of them in tales told around the hearth.

There was another storefront open. A movie theater. Eleanor had started a chain of them. They all showed *Birth of a Nation*, as that was the only full-length movie made yet. Her team managed to put out a new short every two weeks. She also had a serial running with new episodes weekly. They were only fifteen minutes long but were a hit with all the young ladies and their mothers.

Needless to say, they were based on a soap opera with plenty of angst. The women loved it. The men, not so much. Occasionally, you would see some young man escorting his date, but you could tell it was under duress. Some things never change.

We now had our first movie stars as actors and actresses making public appearances at different theaters around the country. None had crossed the channel yet, but it would be big news if they did. I avoided all of it as though it were the plague.

There was beef for sale in the marketplace. It was on ice as we hadn't sorted out refrigeration yet. My large herd was still growing, and I wasn't selling beef yet, but entrepreneur farmers were raising a head or two for the market. The meat was a rare delicacy for this area and sold for a high price.

There was a stall selling used books. These were everything from novels to elementary textbooks. It wouldn't take long for a bookstore to open. I even stopped and talked to the vendor.

I asked him if he had thought of opening a storefront. He had but wasn't selling enough books to pay the rent. I suggested he think about having some tables and chairs so he could sell coffee and some baked goods. He could even have copies of all the regional papers. He could rent them out so he could resell the papers several times over.

He was shaking his head no, but his wife was nodding her head yes. We will have a combination bookstore/coffee shop/news outlet soon. As I started to walk away, I realized I was being unfair to the man and went back.

I wrote him out a note saying I would pay his first six months' rent. If they couldn't make a go of it by then, it wasn't meant to be.

All in all, I was satisfied with the way the economy was improving people's lives and my modernization methods were working.

§ § § §

Liz was cussing up a storm as she helped Bart change the third rubber tire on their five-mile automobile test trip. They had tried to use as little of the precious rubber as possible to make the tires. This was a mistake, as any sharp stone or root would puncture the tire. They would have to make them ten times as thick as these first ones.

Also, if they were thicker, they could try the steel belts mentioned in the literature. This would require several layers of sheet rubber glued together with the crosshatched steel in between. At the same time, they could put water grooves in the tires. These thin balloons they had thought they could save materials with were worthless.

What really irritated her was the small flock of sheep that were being taken to market. This was now the third time they were passing them. The shepherd, at least, had stopped laughing at them. He now kept his eyes straight ahead. She swore that now the sheep were laughing at her.

Liz even thought about buying them at the market so she could eat mutton. That would be a lot of mutton but a satisfying revenge served hot.

Chapter 18

Word from Spain was that the Umayyad Caliphate had defeated the Visigoths at a place called Guadalete, destroying the Visigoths' army and killing the king. For all purposes, the Visigoths were done as a power in Spain. In some ways, this would make it easier for my plans to conquer what I thought of as Spain.

The country would be in disarray for some time to come, and the Umayyad Caliphate wouldn't have time to consolidate its power. I had spies in the area because we knew there would be a battle. The Berbers had been raiding from North Africa for years. Our people at Gibraltar watched inroads being made and reported that things were coming to a head.

The first major battle of the Umayyad conquest of Hispania was the Battle of Guadalete, fought between the Christian Visigoths under their king, Roderic, and the invading forces of the Muslim Umayyad Caliphate, composed mainly of Berbers and some Arabs under the commander Ṭāriq ibn Ziyad. Roderic was killed in the battle, along with many members of the Visigothic nobility, opening the way for the capture of the Visigothic capital of Toledo.

Roderic hadn't been King very long. My spies told me he probably had the last king, Wittiza, assassinated. Between King Achila in the northwest and the Berbers, Roderic never had a chance to completely form an army or control his territory.

The battle of Guadalete was not an isolated Berber attack but followed a series of raids across the Straits of Gibraltar from North

Africa, which resulted in the sack of several south Iberian towns. Berber forces had probably been harassing the peninsula by sea since the conquest of Tangiers.

Two reasonably large armies had been in the south for a year before the decisive battle was fought. Țāriq ibn Ziyad led these.

Țāriq had left from Ceuta in Africa and landed near the Rock of Calpe, also known by us as Gibraltar. Țāriq burned his boats after landing to prevent his army from deserting. From Gibraltar, he moved to conquer the region of Algeciras and then followed the Roman road that led to Seville.

Roderic was fighting the Basques when he was recalled to the south to deal with an invasion. My people had interviewed witnesses to the conflict and had great details on what happened before, during, and after the battle. This information would help us plan our battles with them.

Preceding the battle was an entire week of inconclusive skirmishes near Lake La Janda, in the plain stretching from the Río Barbate.

Țāriq was marching from Cartagena to Córdoba—after defeating a Visigothic army that tried to stop him—when he met Roderic in battle near Shedunya.

Țāriq is said to have landed with 70,000 horsemen and requested 50,000 more from Mūsā. This agreed with my men's estimates of 120,000 Muslim fighters at the battle.

The Visigothic forces were close in size, but the Visigothic kingdom was not organized for war, unlike Francia to its north. There was a small number of elite clans and their warrior followings, the king and his personal following, and the forces that could be raised from the royal fisc constituted the troops upon which Roderic could draw.

The defeat of the Visigothic army followed the flight of the king's opponents, who were supposedly there to help him. Sisibert, an opponent, abandoned Roderic and took the entire right wing of the Visigoth forces with him.

The Muslim army engaged in a series of violent hit-and-run attacks while the Visigothic lines maneuvered in mass. A cavalry wing that had secretly pledged to rebel against Roderic stood aside, giving the enemy an opening.

Ṭāriq's cavalry, the mujaddara, forming as much as a third of the total force and armored in coats of light mail and identifiable by a turban over a metal cap, exploited the opening and charged into the Visigothic infantry, soon followed by Ṭāriq's infantry.

The Christian army was routed, and the king was slain in the final hours of battle. The engagement was a bloodbath: Visigothic losses were extremely high, and the Muslims lost as many as 30,000 men or a quarter of their force.

The Berbers slew the enemies that abandoned Roderic, so Spain was lost for the time being to Christianity. It was my job to take it back. It did seem like the Berbers won, but it was the Visigoths who lost.

The sooner we could bring the Berbers to battle, the better, but I wasn't going to rush in without being completely prepared. We had Santander as a base of operations from the sea and had agreements with the Basque to pass through their mountain passes.

Santander seemed the better option to me. It was also Basque territory but was a different clan than the mountainous ones. If we had to run roughshod over one of them, they would give us the least kickback from the other Basque clans.

We had great stockpiles of munitions, food, and other implements of war. Currently, we estimated that we could field an army of ten thousand for six months. We needed supplies for an army of fifty thousand for a year.

Even with our strong economy and ever-increasing manpower, this goal was straining our supply chain. My staff told me it would be another year before we were ready. This would negate our brief window where the Berbers weren't settled in. I elected to wait rather than rush in without enough men or supplies.

There was no doubt that we would win the war, but I wanted to do it with as few casualties on our side as possible. This included losses from sickness and a poor logistics train. What we could do is start building or improving roads south from Santander. With a year in hand, we could even start a railroad running south. Another item would be to increase our navy to control the sea around Santander and Gibraltar. We needed to prevent reinforcements from arriving once we started fighting.

Our shipbuilding capability had increased dramatically when we opened another shipyard at Saltash. I thought about using Tintagel but was reluctant to do anything to build it back up, giving the old King Geraint supporters a leg up. I guess I did hold a grudge over matters, but so be it.

The new shipyard at Saltash had two drydocks, plus we were building a floating drydock to take care of issues anywhere in the world. To build one of our new ironclads took ten or eleven months so that we could turn out two a year. If push came to shove, once the floating drydock was ready, we could build ships in it.

The land-based drydocks were oversized. They could be used to build ships four times as large as our current vessels. I had hopes of one day even building aircraft carriers. A distant dream but within the world of possibilities.

Our navy would control the seas for the foreseeable future. If I had my way, we would always control the seas.

It was getting close to the time for our annual vacation in our home in Monaco. The weather was turning nasty, so we were anxious to get going on our three-month getaway.

My military advisors always got antsy about these trips, after that time we were ambushed. They would rather we stayed home. That wasn't going to happen. I did make one concession on our itinerary. Instead of going through Arette this year, we would cross the channel and take our train to Paris and from there to Monaco.

This was a new track, so we couldn't have used that route before. A decoy ship would sail as though we were going to use the same route as usual. I thought this was overkill at first but then realized it was my family's safety that was at risk.

Once I got that through my thick skull, the plan came together. We were scheduled to sail from Saltash a week from today. In fact, we will be sailing from London tomorrow. Our train system was the best in the world. Well, it was the only system in the world, though I understood that a group in Gaul was trying to build a steam engine.

We had two sets of my special trains, one in Cornwall and the other in Frankish territory. They were duplicate setups. It was an easy overnight trip to London, and then half a day crossing to Cherbourg. We boarded our train in Cherbourg and spent the night on a siding in Paris as the train was watered and the coal bunker filled.

The train was a familiar sight in Paris, as when I wasn't using it, my officials were allowed to use it on business. There were even some excursions for school kids who were allowed on the train, at least on the public cars. No one was allowed in our private car or the military portion of the train.

The next day, we rolled into Monaco late in the afternoon. All in all, not a bad trip. The kids were old enough now that they weren't a problem about being cooped up. Cathy wrote in her notebook for most of the trip while Doug read. I checked on what Doug was reading.

It was a book written by an independent author of this time period. He had invented Tom Swift or at least a character like him. In the book, Tom invented a lighter-than-air dirigible. Amazing!

I asked Cathy what she was writing, and she told me it was a screenplay for a movie. She wouldn't tell me what the movie was about, but the way she blushed made me think that her mother needed to check this out.

A coach was waiting for us at the train station so we could go straight to our winter home. Eleanor had thought ahead and had ordered that a light evening meal be waiting for us. After that, we all called it an early night. Traveling can be tiring.

The next morning was refreshing. Instead of the dreary weather in Owen-nap, we had fresh air and sunshine. No coats were required, much less hats and gloves.

We had breakfast served on the veranda. Word of our coming had spread, so we had morning visitors. Some were local people we had befriended in previous years. There were a few familiar faces from Cornwall. Since we had chosen this as our winter getaway, others who could afford it did the same.

No doubt, when they got home, they would name-drop, "Yes, we spent time with the earl and his lady."

Since no one was pushy about it, I kept my mouth shut. In the meantime, they would be called snowbirds.

It was nice that Cathy and Doug had friends they could spend time with. Their bodyguards would follow them so they wouldn't get into too much trouble. However, I was beginning to think that Janet Farmer was an enabler. Just what our wild child Cathy needed.

Young love had run its course, so Hagar elected to remain in Owen-nap. He was interested in the new automobile being built, so I had him spend time as a gofer for Bart and Liz. They always needed more hands, so they were glad to have him.

A walk on the beach and lunch, followed by a nap, made the day perfect. That evening we spent listening to the newest records released. The music was getting to be more like what was played in the 1920s and 30s in sound and tempo. It was upbeat and brought a smile to your face. I just hoped it wasn't a precursor to a Great Depression.

The kids invented dances for each type. Eleanor suggested the children invite their friends over for a dance party one night. This great idea proved she was the best mother ever. I grumped a little for form's sake, making me a normal dad.

Each morning, I was brought a daily summary of events in my earldom. All was quiet, with nothing needing my immediate attention. My subordinates were handling things.

This was stacking up to be the best vacation ever.

Chapter 19

The best vacation ever received a puzzling bit of news. Our scouts/spies had run into a group of mercenaries sitting across the border from us. They didn't appear to be doing anything but waiting.

I gave orders that they were to be watched constantly. Mercenaries worked for pay. They didn't sit around doing nothing. There had to be a reason for their presence.

Since they were camped near a small village, it allowed my spies to observe them closely. The villagers came and went from the camp to sell wine and foodstuffs. One of my men was able to go into the camp. His report stated that they were one of the better-known mercenary outfits, the "Black Band".

There were ninety of them. They ran a clean camp and didn't cause trouble with the locals. They were well organized and uniformly outfitted. This placed them uniquely different from most mercenaries. The normal mercenary reputations were of drunken, brawling, slovenly groups.

Of most concern was that there were only ninety of them. According to my spies, their companies had one hundred men. Where were the other ten?

Taking no chances, I had everyone put on alert. Our personal bodyguards were doubled up, and patrols of the area were made twice as often. This went on for a week. Like any alert situation, men and women began to tire. When nothing appeared to be happening, I ordered everyone to stand down and return to our normal level of vigilance.

That proved to be a mistake. The mercenaries were professionals and had played us. By setting up camp where they could be easily found, they had alarmed us. We reacted predictably by stepping up our security. When my people were tired and had to be stepped down, they struck.

Those missing ten men had been hidden in an abandoned farmhouse not far from our home. They had been waiting for an opportunity to kidnap one of my family. My son Doug needed to get out and exercise after being locked down for a week. He went riding along with three bodyguards.

Their hiding place was well chosen as Doug and his little troop would ride past the building. It was in between two small hills, so out of sight of the main village. We had manned watch towers on the outskirts of the village, but for about ten minutes, Doug and his bodyguards would be out of sight behind the hills.

One of the watchmen had been keeping track of Doug and his riders, and when they didn't come into sight when he expected, he watched for a few more minutes and then rang his alarm bell.

My people had learned that they would never be penalized for acting when they had suspicions. His were well-founded. As he was sounding the alarm, a larger group of riders emerged on the far side of the hill, riding at a fast trot to the border.

When our patrol reached the valley between the hills, they found the bodies of Doug's guards. They had been ambushed by men using modern crossbows.

The patrol rode after the kidnappers until they came to the border. The border wasn't well marked, but they knew the general demarcation between France and Italy, my names for the two areas.

The only reason they didn't follow the kidnappers into Italy was that the Black Band had moved up so their ten missing members could rejoin them. Now, the patrol went from twenty against ten to twenty against one hundred.

They wisely backed down. Riding back to inform me of what was happening, they left four men behind to shadow them. This was dangerous for those men as the Black Band would know they were being shadowed and leave ambushers behind to kill my scouts.

In conference with Eleanor and the brigadier general in command of the five hundred troops who were providing local security, I expressed my concern about the scouts.

The general spoke up, "My Lord James, we have been experimenting with a new method of scouting in situations like this."

"What is that?" I asked.

"We use observation balloons advancing one after another. You might say we leapfrog them."

I had introduced leapfrogging on one of my school visits. It proved popular even with young men. As many as fifty of them would create a train of them across the countryside. The young ladies loved it.

"How does that work?" Eleanor asked.

"We will move a balloon within ten miles of their camp. They only push their rear scouts out five miles from what our people are reporting. We raise the balloon and from there can observe their next thirty miles of progress with telescopes."

The general continued, "While that balloon is observing, another is in a cart being pulled by mules so they can make good time. The cart can move faster than the mercenaries and their camp followers, so when they pitch camp that evening, we move up to within ten miles of them. Thus, we can watch their route and where their scouts plan for them to follow the next day."

"Excellent," I replied, "Let's do that. We can't leave this area undefended as this may only be a feint to drive deeper into our territory. Follow on with two hundred troops and their attached cannon. In the meantime, I'm going to have five thousand more troops assemble here to follow on as needed."

"Why so many, My Lord Earl?"

"I'm sick and tired of these plots. We are going to follow the mercenaries, take them, find out who is paying them, and take them down."

Eleanor added, "Take them down hard. That is my son they are playing their game with."

"Yes, dear, very hard."

We continued with our planning.

"Since we will know the route they are planning for the next day, we can send a force around them and wait for them at a defendable spot. They will be the anvil. The following force will be the hammer."

We decided that a mounted force of fifty men could circle past the mercenaries and set up a roadblock ahead of them.

It took time to get orders issued and men moving, so it was the next day before a force of two hundred men set out, fifty to get ahead of the raiders and one hundred and fifty to follow them.

The balloons had an escort of twenty-five men each. They were in radio contact with us so they could see and report any trouble coming their way.

The balloons set out that night. Their escort had lanterns to light their way. We had some concern that light from the lanterns would reflect off the clouds and notify the enemy of our presence. It turned out to be a cloudless night, and the light couldn't be discerned more than three miles away, so we decided to chance it.

The balloons were within ten miles of the camp at daybreak, and we launched the first balloon shortly after that. A balloonist reported by radio that Doug was kept in a cage mounted on a wagon. They saw that he was let out to eat and use their latrines. He wasn't being mistreated.

This meant they might be allowed to live.

The balloon watchers also reported the raiders were following an old Roman road due south along the coast. Our fifty-man force moved further inland ten miles, then turned south. Without pushing their mounts, they kept up a steady pace and soon drew even with, then passed, the mercenary raiders.

The mercenaries and their camp followers looked to be making fifteen miles a day. Our forward force could do twenty and even twenty-five miles as they had no encumbrances. Our follow-on force with cannon could do fifteen to eighteen miles daily, so we had them boxed in.

While this was going on that first day, I was sending out messages ordering five thousand men to be brought in by train along with all their equipment and no camp followers! This practice had to be stopped. I also realized that this would only prevent families from following.

The whores, merchants, and swindlers would come no matter what. At least they would try to follow us. No trains would be made available. Guards at each station would block their progress. I was introducing the concepts of twenty-first-century warfare.

Since we were a mobile force, we would do our own camp security, cleaning, and food preparation. In the future, we will need civilian contractors to provide those services in a fixed base camp. Unlike World War II and Korea, men were to concentrate on being fighters. It costs a lot of money to train a soldier. I didn't want to waste it on them being cooks if I didn't have to.

By the third day, one of the balloons reported there was a river crossing ahead, which had a bridge. This would be an ideal spot to stop the mercenaries.

The mounted troops rode up to the river before they turned towards the coast. Following the river, they soon found the bridge. They hadn't cut over to the Roman road before this, as the passing of fifty horses wouldn't go unnoticed.

By the time the mercenaries reached the bridge, it would be too late. Our following force picked up the pace and was in position to attack the mercenaries on my command.

When the mercenary scouts reported the roadblock up ahead, the main body stopped. I had my forces move up to them. We almost had to shove the camp followers out of our way to reach the main body.

Fifty of our men did move the camp followers aside. After the followers were safely out of the way, twenty-five men stayed behind to keep the followers in place. The rest rejoined the main force.

As my men and cannon formed a line facing the mercenaries, I had a white flag on a banner brought forward. Along with ten men as bodyguards, I advanced towards the mercenaries. Stopping out of crossbow reach, I waited. Our scouts and balloonists hadn't reported any longbows.

It didn't take long before a party under a white flag left the raiders assembled before us. They were led by a hard-bitten-looking leader. His weathered features spoke of many years in the field. His scarred face spoke of many battles.

He didn't believe in pleasantries.

"We have your son, and he will die if you attack us."

"If my son dies, you, your men, and all the camp followers will join him."

"Bold words. We are almost even in fighters, so you might just lose that battle."

I had prepared for this eventuality. I raised my arm and chopped it down. One cannon fired into the forest, lining the road. Loaded with canister, it cleared the underbrush and felled several of the smaller trees.

I raised my arm and brought it down once more, and my men on this side of the river fired five rapid gunshots into the air. Another arm motion brought the same from the other side of the river.

I now smiled grimly at the mercenary captain.

"I believe we have proven we can do as I say. Now, I will pay you five thousand silver for my son and the name of the person who hired you."

The captain responded slowly, so I raised my arm once more. The cannon, loaded with a ball, fired and knocked down a large tree.

This time, the captain quickly accepted my offer. I had a chest brought forward that contained the silver coins. My son was reunited with his mother. At that age, he didn't want public displays of affection, such as hugs from his parents. This time, he clung to her.

"Who hired you?"

"The College of Cardinals want revenge for your handling of one of their own."

"You mean the one that was poisoned?"

"That doesn't matter to them."

"There is one more matter to be settled. Your men killed three of mine."

Chapter 20

The mercenary captain looked at me like I had two heads.

"They were only soldiers. They are disposable. Why are you concerned about them?"

He didn't even care that he was saying that in front of his own men.

I replied, "So even your men are just pawns to be used?"

"They don't even rank as well as pawns."

His men didn't seem to be too upset at his attitude. The captain must have made his feelings known many times.

The captain continued, "As long as they get paid, they don't care what happens to each other or even me. They are out for themselves."

"That brings me back to my point. I do care about my men and want compensation for their families."

"How much are you asking?"

"I think five thousand silver will do."

His eyes got wide.

"I need that money to pay my men."

"Didn't you get paid in advance by the cardinals?"

"Yes, but I had some debts that had to be paid. I will give you one hundred silver for each of your three men."

I pretended to think for a moment.

"No, that won't do. They were well-trained, loyal soldiers. They are worth five thousand silver."

"I'm not giving it to you."

At that, he turned to his men and told them to take the chest away. They started for it.

In a conversational voice, I told them, "Touch that chest, and I will order the cannon to open fire."

The captain told them, "Take it. He won't do anything."

The captain's men stood there, not knowing what to do. The captain, in a rage, pulled his sword. I thought he was going to go after his men. Instead, he lunged at me.

He didn't complete his lunge. Apparently, he didn't understand what firearms could do. My guards had had their pistols out the whole time and pointed at him. Before he could push the sword towards my middle, four shots rang out. All hit him center mass. As he hit the ground, another four shots rang out. They were following procedure with a shot to his head. Before they could pull the trigger for a double tap, I told them to halt.

I asked the mercenaries standing there open-mouthed, "Who is next in command?"

They pointed towards a sturdy-looking man.

"Antonio is our lieutenant."

I asked, "Antonio, how much are your men owed?"

"Altogether, five hundred silver for the last month."

"Line your people up. I will pay them what they are owed. Plus, I will provide you another one thousand to tide you over until your next job."

"That is more than kind of you, My Lord Earl."

One of the mercenaries ran to a mule that had several saddlebags tied to it. He returned with a large ledger book. It seemed that this was a well-organized group.

A table and campstool were brought up from the camp followers. They were updated on events by the runner who went for the table and chairs.

I didn't hear any moaning about the captain's fate. Either these people were as heartless as the captain told me, or they hated him. I would bet on hate.

With two of my people overseeing the disbursement, I checked out the saddlebags on the mule. I found five coded messages. The code was in blocks of five digits. NSA could have figured it out in minutes, but I didn't have a supercomputer, so I was stuck.

There was also a book from Archbishop Luke's printing press. It was on how to make a hothouse. It was a short book of forty pages.

It dawned on me that the code being used was a book cipher. The people sending the messages had identical books, down to the particular edition.

With a book cipher, you would replace the numbers with a letter. The letter would be found by first using the first number to tell the page, then the paragraph, then the line finally, the first letter of the word found in the numbered position.

It took some fiddling as some page numbers were only one digit rather than two. They used a small book to keep the number of page references down. Some of the letters only required four digits. I quickly found they used a zero as the last digit if only four digits were required. This was poor tradecraft, but I wasn't complaining.

For example, if "apple" appears on page 42, line 3, word 5, you'd encode it as 42-3-5.

After an hour of working with the cipher, I had decoded the five short messages. It turned out the mercenary captain had lied to me. On his real master's orders, that was the answer he was to give if questioned.

The truth was he was working for the Byzantine Emperor. At least now, I didn't have to conquer Rome, which was for later.

With our son retrieved, my small army started back to Monaco. The mercenary group headed towards Rome. As the camp followers passed us on their way south, I heard many of them blessing me for my mercy, both in letting them live and getting rid of the hated captain.

I didn't understand why they hadn't assassinated him themselves but didn't care enough to ask.

Once back in Monaco, I sent a radio message ordering five thousand silver to be provided appropriately to the surviving families of the three men who were murdered. I didn't go into detail about how it was to be divided. There could be an easy situation: a wife with children. Or a bachelor soldier with parents and/or brothers and sisters. That was Thad's headache.

Once I was back at our home in Monaco, I had time to think. The messages made it clear that the captain's debts had been bought up by the emperor's people. They would consider them paid along with ten thousand silver if they could deliver one of my family members to the docks in Ostia by a certain date. The date was a month from now, so we had plenty of time to put my plan in place.

We had the name of the ship and the password to let them know we were the Black Band mercenaries and were successful in our mission. Our only time constraint was the mercenaries reaching Rome and the word of their failure getting out.

An armed schooner left Gibraltar with fifty armsmen on board. They were able to reach Ostia in five days. They waited on a tide that occurred in the nighttime before docking. A bribe in hand to the port authority told them where the Byzantine ship was docked. Five of our armsmen openly approached the ship. They had a rug wrapped around a small log about the size of a young man.

The other forty-five were stationed out of sight. Five of them were watching for unwanted visitors; the rest were ready to rush the ship.

A man stationed at the ship's gangway demanded who the men getting ready to board were. They gave the password and were told to come back in the daytime.

Our man, who had gone up the gangway to give the password, then stabbed the guard in the stomach. The in-shock man was pushed overboard to either drown or bleed out.

The party's leader signaled, and our entire force, except for our watchmen, quickly boarded the ship. There were few crew on board. Our spies had reported that the ship's officers and most of the crew were staying at inns on their extended stay.

It didn't take long for the crew to be subdued. Some tried to fight and paid the ultimate price. Those who surrendered were bound and set on the deck under guard.

The next step was a thorough search of the ship. A large chest with the money promised to the Black Band mercenaries was found and transported to our ship.

In the captain's quarters, documents and further valuables in the form of gold bars and gems were found. The ship did have a small cargo of silk from the Orient. All of this was moved to our ship.

Casks of oil were brought on board and poured everywhere. The bound sailors were taken ashore and left bound far enough away they wouldn't burn with the ship.

Torches were lit and thrown onto the ship, which, like all wooden vessels, started to burn brightly. Luckily for the Romans, no other ships were docked near the burning vessel. If they had, it would have been their bad luck.

My men boarded the schooner and watched as word of the fire spread. There was nothing to be done, so the huge crowd who gathered watched the Byzantine ship burn to the water line.

As soon as the tide turned, our schooner sailed from Ostia, heading to Saltash. The documents captured contained codes for passing messages back to Constantinople. Over the open radio waves, we sent a message to the emperor using his code. It simply told him there would be a price for his actions.

I hadn't decided what the price would be, but it wouldn't be killing any of his family members. I had a brilliant thought and signaled the emperor that none of his ships, military or civilian, would be allowed past the Straits of Gibraltar.

Any ship attempting would be either seized or sunk. I issued orders to the fort at Gibraltar to that effect. We held Gibraltar, but the Moors were landing twenty miles along the coast. We didn't have the manpower to stop them.

Word was received from the expedition to Guinea that they had found a harbor that met our requirements of having a high area nearby to avoid the diseases that plagued the African coast.

Not only that, but they also identified a source of bauxite not too far away with a fast-flowing river within two miles.

I found this to be very exciting. After letting my advisors know my plans, I had a small fleet of four cargo ships and two armed schooners readied to set out.

The cargo ships carried miners and a turbine-powered electrical generator. I was anxious to get my hands on some aluminum. It wouldn't be a large-scale operation, but they would be able to ship back over one hundred tons of aluminum ingots.

When I told Eleanor about my plans, she asked if I planned to house and feed my miners. Oops! Another four ships were added to the convoy and two more escorts.

I slowed my efforts down and actually listened to my advisors this time instead of telling them. A construction crew was added to build docks and a fort to guard the harbor.

Instead of adding more ships, we delayed sending the miners until the basic infrastructure was in place. The cargo ships would deliver the first group and then return for the second.

Eleanor asked me, "Why are you in such a hurry all of a sudden?"

"Bart and Liz have a working internal combustion engine. It is too heavy for use in a dirigible. With aluminum, we can make lighter engines to propel the aircraft."

"Are these machines useful, other than not needing to follow roads?"

"They will be able to move through the air forty or fifty miles an hour. More if the prevailing wind is behind them. Think of boarding such an aircraft here in Owen-nap and arriving in Monaco twenty hours later with a good night's sleep along the way. No rattling train cars."

I didn't mention the airships' noisy engines.

I continued, "Also, they can be used as a weapon of war. They can haul tons of bombs. We can drop the bombs on troops below us and never be in danger."

"That doesn't seem fair."

"War isn't fair. We are going to need this advantage when we go into Spain. The Moors will have a quarter million men or more. Right now, we can field seventy thousand. Even with our cannons and rifles, we would soon be overrun."

"When you say 'we,' do you mean that you will be with your army?"

"Yes, dear, I must lead my men into a battle this large."

"Then get this new metal here as fast as you can."

"Yes, dear."

Chapter 21

Arne Pedersen, the eyewitness of the count's murder in Jutland, was following his uncle's footsteps in going to sea. He had accompanied me to Cornwall for his safety. Even though that threat had been resolved, he kept putting off going home.

Instead, he spent his time at the docks in Saltash. He talked to every returning sailor about their voyages. He wanted to know about the practical aspects of the trip, not the fun times in port.

He finally asked to see me and to get permission to join the Navy. Our navy, the Royal Cornwall Navy, or RCN, was a small group with twelve ships at sea and two others being built. Those at sea were armed schooners except for our single metal-hulled, screw-powered ship.

The two under construction were armored steam-powered vessels. These had improvements based on knowledge gained from the first vessel's time at sea. I asked Arne if he had his parents' permission. He told me he had written them, and they told him it was all right with them even though he was old enough to make his own decisions.

Based on that, I commissioned Arne as an ensign in our new navy. We were so new we didn't even have any midshipmen yet.

This explained how Arne was on board our steam-powered ship on its way to Guinea. I had been on the radio so much and was such a pain to the expedition's leaders that Eleanor told me to leave the house and go there. I would still be a pain, but it would be a pain in Africa. There must be a bad joke in there somewhere.

It was a quick trip with us only stopping at Gibraltar as a courtesy visit and refueling. The rock rats, as they called themselves, were tunneling ever deeper into the mountain. It would be a fortress like no other in the world.

I think the commander dragged me through every inch of every tunnel. They had done an impressive job and had enough stores on hand to hold off a one-hundred-year siege. Maybe not that long, but a long time. When I mentioned that, I was told that they had finally got the ten years' worth of supplies they wanted and that now they could release shipments to the depot in Santander.

That's when I twigged that the buildup in Santander was behind because the army had been diverting supplies from Santander to here. This is why I was losing my chance to hit the Moors before they had a chance to settle in. I had to ask for a few minutes in private. I was fit to burst and didn't want to take any actions I might regret later, such as killing this idiot of a commander.

After counting to one hundred, five times slowly, I realized that even if I had the supplies, I didn't have the manpower to attack the Moors at this time. Once that became clear to me, I decided to let it go. What was done was done, and now the real build-up can start.

That evening there was a dinner held in honor of my visit. I said all good things about their progress. Upon more mature thought, I realized that it was more important to hold this choke point than to prematurely attack the Moors in Spain.

The commander and his officer told me how they were blockading the Byzantines from the strait and that they were sinking everyone who tried to pass.

The next morning, before we set sail, I was taken to the highest point on the rock. Through a telescope, I watched a Byzantine ship try to run the strait. Our cannon reached out ten miles and hit the ship squarely amidships.

I praised the gun crew for their accuracy. One old hand spoke up, "Sheer luck, My Lord. This is the first one that we have managed to hit in three days."

From his officer's sour looks, I knew this to be the truth.

I replied, "Still, that was good shooting. It will make the Byzantine ships reluctant to try the straits. Their owners won't like the losses."

I turned to the officer in charge of the battery.

"Give this gun crew an extra tot tonight. I need to hear the truth of matters. If it ever comes to my attention that this man was punished for telling it, there will be hell to pay.

"On second thought, he will come with me. We always need good gunners on our ship."

As he passed me to get his gear, the gunner said, "Thank you, My Lord; it would have been my death if you had left me here."

At the dock, the commander and his senior officers were there to see me off. Last night at dinner, they were sitting down, and I had retired to my room immediately after. Now I noticed how portly a group they were. These didn't look like fighting men.

We set sail shortly after that. Once at sea, I sent a coded message to CIA headquarters asking for an undercover investigation of the officer corps in Gibraltar. Something wasn't right.

I interviewed the gunner from the rock.

"Now that we have you away from there, please tell me what is happening with the officers."

"They are as corrupt as they come. They won't let us practice our gunnery because they sell gunpowder to the Moors. If we had the new shells, they would be selling them also."

I was puzzled, "Why would the Moors buy gunpowder?"

The gunner looked at me like I was a lackwit.

"For the cannon that they have sold them."

I radioed Cornwall and told the CIA that I wanted a full inventory of the cannon and gunpowder shipped to Gibraltar. If what the man was telling me was true, people would hang.

There was nothing more I could do at this point as we cruised on to Guinea. We had been given clear information on where the new harbor was situated. The longitude and latitude points were of some use, but our clocks didn't have the accuracy yet for point-to-point navigation. It would get us into the proper area, and then we had to search out the landmarks. A meeting at sea would be a problem.

There, the ships would get into the region and then take turns firing cannons. This method worked but was burdensome. I called it the "Can you hear me now?" method. I had people working on better timepieces.

Once we made landfall, I was impressed at how much progress the advance team had made. Pilings had been driven for a dock to be built. We had to use the ship's boat to go ashore, but that would be rectified in a few days.

Once ashore, it was hot and humid. We had the sea breeze before to keep us cool, but now it was almost unbearable. There were bugs everywhere, and some I swear could have picked me up and carried me away. The engineers assured me they sprayed DDT in every low spot in the area. All places with standing water were scheduled to be filled in.

The harbor was towered over by a high prominence. It was over two hundred feet above sea level. A rough path had been laid out to the top. To reach the top, you had to go inland a quarter mile, then go another quarter mile up a ridge to the top. A crew was working on turning the path into a road.

The top of the prominence was relatively flat and covered several hundred acres. Surveyors had laid out a small village to start. The prominence had a small woods which was marked for preservation. This was to be a park area.

On top, the sea breeze made the temperature more than comfortable. It was heaven when compared with down below. This made me even more determined to develop air conditioning.

My engineers told me that once the docks were complete and the mosquitoes and other bugs were under control, most work in the dock would be performed after dark. Electric lights would be used so the area would be lit like daylight.

I had been concerned with how we would stand off any attacks from shore. Now that I saw what we had, there was no problem. A wall with gates blocking access to the top of the promontory with several cannon batteries would make the place unassailable.

I asked about the water supply. There was a natural spring on top, but it didn't have enough flow rate to meet our needs.

"My Lord, we will run a pipe to the river you see down below. It is fresh water. The pipe will be buried, and the inlet will be underwater."

"Do we have a pump that can pull water this high?"

"Not yet, but one will be on the next shipload of materials. We also plan to build a large cistern to catch and store rainwater."

"All good. How do you plan to power the pump?"

"The whole infrastructure will be powered by an electric turbine."

"What will power the turbine?"

"The excess water pumped up will fall through a tube with the turbine mounted inside. We have enough head pressure to provide electricity for all that we have planned here."

"I authorize you to duplicate the entire water and power setup here. A system failure would be a disaster."

"Thank you, My Lord."

One thing I haven't asked is what are you going to name this settlement?"

"The men had a contest, and 'Earl's Point' won."

"Oh."

What do you say to that?

The engineer took me to the highest point on the headland.

"We intend to build a one-hundred-foot-tall combination watchtower and lighthouse here."

"Who thought of that? It wasn't in our plans, but it is a wonderful idea."

The engineer, Jan Broekman, blushed and said, "I did, My Lord. With telescopes, we will be able to see ships over fifty miles away."

I looked around and saw a nearby surveying team with their rods. I borrowed one and knighted him as Sir Broekman. Using nearby implements became a norm for me and a point of pride for the new knights.

At dinner that night, set up on trestle tables under torchlight, I was able to ask some more questions.

"Have we run into any of the local natives yet?"

"Yes, we have. We interrupted a group of slave raiders attacking the locals. We now have excellent relations, and they are interested in our work. They see it as an opportunity to better themselves."

"Good, I want to make this very clear: we aren't enslaving them or treating them as second-rate citizens. What we are building here is not to take advantage of them. They will be treated as citizens of Cornwall."

I continued, "I will have the grey ladies set up Mash units for them. As things progress their children will be educated. Our religion will not be forced on them. Am I clear?"

"Yes, My Lord."

"Good, as the first governor of Earl's Point, it is your duty to make it so."

I love springing surprises like that on people.

The next day, with a large armed escort, I was shown the bauxite deposit that had been found. Not that far away was a fast-flowing river. I asked what the natives called it.

"Fast flowing river."

"That won't do. Hold a naming contest for it. Just don't use mine again."

The bauxite deposit had been sampled, but there was no way of knowing how large it was until mining started. That would be a while. I hoped it would be enough to make a dozen or so aircraft engines.

Roads were being laid out from the deposit to the river and back to our little port.

While we were examining the area, we were approached by several natives. We hadn't established a common language yet, but they didn't hesitate to put down two blankets and several gourds.

At first, I thought they were trying to sell us food, but as one of them pulled the top off the gourd, I realized it was being used as a container.

He reached into the gourd and picked up a handful of raw gold.

Chapter 22

I t was a lot of gold. There must have been twenty pounds of it. I wondered what they wanted in trade. We weren't at our camp where our trade goods were kept, so we didn't have a lot to offer.

It became clear in a moment what they wanted, as their leader pointed at a rifle. I said no loudly and shook my head no at the same time. He got the message.

The leader started making motions to indicate multiple gourds. I think he was offering even more for the rifle. Again, I said no. You didn't need a common language to know he was disappointed.

I didn't feel threatened by his disappointment. I held out my steel machete for him to examine. He took it, tested the sharpness of the blade with his thumb, and then took a swing at a nearby bush. When it cut through the bush easily, he smiled and measured some gold out on a large leaf.

He was offering a pound of gold for the machete. That was way too much. I picked another leaf of the same size. I think they were called elephant ears. I divided the gold into two piles. I laid my machete on top of his leaf. I held out my hand to one of my escorts for his machete. I then laid that knife on the second pile of gold.

With a large smile, the leader picked up both knives. In turn, I signaled for one of my men to collect the gold. It took further hand signaling to make him understand that he and his companions were to follow us.

It only took us a half hour to return to the dock area where our trading goods were kept. We had mirrors, machetes, and sundry other goods. The chief was only interested in the knives and mirrors.

It didn't take long for him to trade for all of our knives and two mirrors. This was one of those times that both sides thought they had got the better of the deal.

As they turned to go, I stopped them. I picked up a glass bead necklace and put it around one of my female guard's necks. I then handed him another one. I don't know if he got the idea that it was a present for his wife or not, but he took it and didn't wear it himself.

When they left, I voiced the thought that we had to find some way to communicate with them. My new governor, Sir Broekman, told me there might be a way.

"We have some prisoners from the Arab slave raiders. Maybe one of them can talk to them."

At the prison enclosure, I asked loudly if anyone spoke Latin. Two men volunteered that they did. I asked if they could communicate with the natives. They couldn't, but one of their party could.

This would be difficult, but it might work. I would ask a question in Latin to the Arabs, and they, in turn would ask it to the native speaker, who would then ask the native my question. Even if done in good faith, there would be a lot of room for error.

There was a pleasant surprise at dinner that night. I was explaining about our translation problems. A lieutenant spoke up.

"Sir, my Arabic is pretty good, if that would help."

"A Godsend is what it is."

I had a thought.

"I want you to listen in to our first attempts to see if the two Latin-speaking Arabs are being honest with us."

The next morning, I had the two Latin speakers and the native language speakers brought together as a test as I told them to see how this would work.

I told the Latin speakers in Latin that I wished to have honest trade with the natives and that we wouldn't be pulling any tricks.

After I spoke, the three Arabs talked among themselves.

The lieutenant spoke up, "Sir, they are trying to figure out how to steal any gold we have and escape."

"Tell them that is not a good idea and have the two Latin speakers taken back to the prison."

Turning to the governor, I asked, "What will we do with the prisoners? We can't hold them long term."

"I thought we would hand them over to the natives they tried to enslave."

"That's a good idea. It gets them out of our hair, shows the locals we understand their need for revenge."

The governor laughed, "And saves us the cost of good rope."

The captain of my guards broke in, "Why use a good rope when you have a cliff handy?"

That made us roar with laughter once again. This was a harsh day and age we lived in.

We did turn the Arabs over to the locals, and the locals surprised us. We thought they would kill them. Instead, they put them to work clearing fields for more crops. Even more surprising, I was told that the Arabs could work their way out of slavery over a long period of time. They could even marry local women.

I asked the chief if he was worried if they would run and he told me they were welcome to try. The jungle was dangerous, not only because of the animals but other tribes.

The Arabs must have known this because they all settled into their new lives. Every time I thought I understood people, I was shown to be wrong.

I did have a radio message sent ordering the next ships to have machetes, shovels, hoes, axes, pots, pans, and any other metalware that might be of use here.

With the natives bringing gold to trade, we wouldn't have to placer mine or dig tunnels. We would let them do the work.

After all, this was their land, and why shouldn't they get something out of all this? It also meant I had to stop charging half a pound of gold for a machete. For that price, they should get one hundred of them.

That reminded me I had to talk to the chief about the concept of land ownership and the mining of minerals. If they were to be absorbed into my realm, they needed to be treated fairly at the start.

After I had that thought, I remembered I had left a Native American in Cornwall. I needed to see if he had learned enough Cornish to have the same conversation with him.

It was a torturous process working with two middlemen doing the translation. It is a wonder we didn't set off a war. Occasionally, the message I was trying to tell the chief would set him off laughing. It was the same the other way. I think it was these obvious errors that made it work.

I stayed for ten days. During that time, our next supply ship came in. It had the hundreds of farm implements that I had requested. This included a thousand machetes.

When we laid the blankets out to trade, the first thing I did was put down one hundred of the knives and one pound of gold beside them. With our clumsy translation, it took a while, but I got the message across that this was the real price of the knives. I then gave him the gold from the first trade, and we started over.

We had laid out twenty blankets for this session. It was just as well because the chief had brought most of his tribe along.

His wife was there, and I was pleased to see that she was wearing the necklace that I had given her husband. When the chief realized how rich his people really were, he promptly bought everything laid out.

Once that trade was completed, I had a case of necklaces opened. These were the same quality as the first one presented but a little different. I gave one out to every male present, including the chief. This meant his wife now had two necklaces. I wondered if I had started "keeping up with the Jones".

Every husband present was smart enough to hand a necklace to their wife. This left a group of single men facing single women. The young lady's mothers joined the girls, and rapid-fire talk commenced. I couldn't follow it, but I think I had just set off a marriage mart.

This was confirmed when a young man approached a young lady and presented his necklace to her. She let out a squeal as she nodded her head yes. He put it around her neck and hugged her. They left the clearing hand in hand. I think they had just gotten married.

This occurred several more times until there were only a few couples left. Nothing more happened as the men put their necklaces away. It seems the brides weren't acceptable to them.

One young lady in tears held out her arms to a young man, but he turned his back on her. She was attractive, so I didn't understand why he rejected her.

Later conversation would reveal that while pretty, she was poor and wouldn't bring much of a dowry. He had been dating her and leading her on with no intention of marrying her.

She started to walk away dejectedly when one of my road workers caught up with her. She stopped, and while they didn't have a common language, they communicated. He went down on one knee and presented her with three necklaces.

She couldn't get them on fast enough. He then sealed the deal with a kiss. From the oohs and aahs from the crowd, this wasn't done, or at least not in public.

One thing I had noticed was that this tribe was monogamous. I didn't know how this would work with other tribes, but that was a problem for another day.

After my road worker and his bride returned from their trip to the bushes, I had a chance to ask him why he did it.

"My Lord, I was intending to stay here anyway. I have thought about it and realized that taking a local wife would be a good idea. I have no family waiting in Cornwall, so I decided to go for it. When the prettiest girl in Africa is available, why not?"

The young man who had rejected the young lady now had problems of his own. He tried to present a necklace to one of the remaining girls, and she turned him down. He then made a fatal mistake, at least in the matrimony market. He turned to a second lady and presented his necklace. She turned him down.

He was ready to go to a third young lady when he saw they all had turned their backs on him. The rest of the tribe, the sensitive souls that they were, all laughed at him.

Since this trading session was to be a landmark in opening our relations with a different group, I had a radio set up with an announcer giving a play-by-play of the day's events. I thought it would be the trading that he would talk about. He did, but he also gave a play-by-play broadcast of the entire handing-out necklace event, including the rejection and subsequent marriage and the following rejection of the young man who had scorned the bride.

Of course, recordings were kept of the broadcast, which was played over and over in all my territories. The road worker was an instant standard for men's behavior. The young lady, a poor girl, made a good heroine. As far as the young man who did the rejection, he might as well move to another tribe far away.

Two weeks later a short movie was being shown in every theater of the events of that day. The only oddity was that all the actors were white. They were dressed as the natives were in the movie, but it looked strange to me when I saw it later.

Chapter 23

I avidly kept track of the progress of our operations in Guinea. I was also updated on Sir Barts and Dame Liz's progress on the automobile, especially the engine portion.

We had a prototype airship in the air. It was powered by a small steam engine. We had taken great precautions so that there would be no loose sparks. On top of that, there were multiple hydrogen balloon sacks installed in rubber-coated sheet metal containers.

All metal used was bronze, which wouldn't spark. All personnel wore one-piece uniforms with no metal buttons. They had special shoes that had bronze nails in the heels. When we had aluminum available, it would replace all bronze.

Safety training on the consequences of the hydrogen being lit off was emphasized. Demonstrations were given of the explosive burning of hydrogen. We had several people drop out of training in fear. We also kicked out five men for being careless in their actions. One of them even lit up his pipe on board. His crewmates almost threw him out at five hundred feet.

We implemented a new rule: no smokers were allowed in the program. We lost another three people but even they agreed it was the right thing. They were given administrative jobs on the ground, so they didn't suffer too much.

The prototype was so successful that I approved the production of a full-sized airship. Once the bugs were worked out of the new aircraft, I intended to have a fleet of ten dirigibles.

Another project was being worked on in our remote explosive laboratory. Their mission was to develop a fuel-air bomb. Nasty, but the only way we could face an army of a quarter-million men.

One evening I had a serious conversation with Eleanor.

"Dear, I have to decide what sort of government we should have in the long run."

"I don't understand; you're the government."

"What about after I die?"

"Cathy will take over. We have already discussed this."

"After her?"

"Her eldest, of course."

"What if that child is weak of mind?"

"Then the child will have to have a regent."

"In all the history that I have read, that is where things go wrong. Everything from the regent trying to seize power by killing the child to corrupting the child."

I then gave her the example of Ivan the Terrible and how he was raised.

"This is the weakness of our form of government. One poor leader and things go wrong. Sometimes the country can survive it, but usually there is a lot of pain and suffering along the way."

"What works?"

"We don't know. In all of history, no form of government has done well for more than two hundred years."

"We will be long dead by then, so why worry?"

"I would like to leave a better world for our descendants. To do that, we must set up the mechanism in our lifetime."

"What has worked best in history?"

"A republic or a parliamentary system."

I then explained how each worked. The republic seemed to be the best though it was far from perfect. I was careful to keep separate a republic from a democracy. I agreed with Jefferson that when people learned they could vote themselves money it would be the beginning of the end for the country as he knew it.

"Dear, what are the weaknesses of a republic?"

"When the elected officials have to spend more time getting ready for the next election than doing their duty. They must raise funds for the election. This means that large donors have a stronger voice than the people. These donors may be rich people or lobbyists for industries."

This led to an explanation of what a lobbyist was and how industries would try to sway the laws in their favor.

"How would you fix this?"

"It has been suggested that term limits would be the solution, though it hasn't been tried. The thought is that if a person couldn't be in an elected office for more than several terms, they wouldn't have time to be corrupted or have to worry about continuously having to raise money."

I continued, "This leads to only rich people running for office, which has its own problems.

"Another weakness of a republic is the bureaucracy. Politicians spend so much time running for office that the bureaucrats set the rules and are the real power. They are hired for the job and have no term limits."

"Why not give them term limits?"

"Experience does count. It has been suggested but not tried to not let the bureaucrats be in the same place as the governing officials."

"What do you mean?"

"For example, the treasury run by bureaucrats would be here. The politicians would work from London. The War Department from another town, the Department of Agriculture could be in Paris, and so on.

"In my country, we have a Senate and a House. The Senate had longer terms than the House. The house was the voice of the people and controlled the purse. The Senate was originally set up to be the voice of the individual states. This devolved into a democratic election.

"There would be two senators from each state or county as we know them. The house would have members representing so many people. This setup gave the smaller states or counties a voice. These two groups would vote on the laws of the land.

"There was a constitution which set up the original guiding laws, but it could be amended at need.

"A supreme court would decide if a law passed met the constitution's requirements."

There is a third branch, the executive branch, headed by an elected leader. This leader would run the bureaucracy and the nation as a whole during times of war. Though war could only be declared by the two houses of Congress."

"That sounds so complicated; how could it work?"

"It wasn't meant to. The people who wrote the constitution didn't trust any single group to work in the best interests of the country, so they set it up so that the various branches would always be at loggerheads."

"What's a loggerhead?"

"In this case, always in conflict."

And another word appears in our language.

Eleanor asks, "So what do you think we should do?"

"Right now, I'm leaning towards moving the bureaucracy to different locations. Having a House of Lords comprised of the head of each county and an elected House of Representatives which would devise the budget. The Lords would approve it. A constitution, and a supreme court."

"What about you?"

"I would be the executive officer with a veto power over everything, plus control of the bureaucrats."

"What about the line of succession?"

"It would remain the same with the exception that the Congress could vote out a person unable to lead. This would require a ninety percent vote so that it couldn't be done lightly."

"What about a child who is too young to lead but inherits the position?"

"A regent appointed and removed by the Congress. Again, a majority vote. The regency not to last beyond the child's coming of age."

"What if there is no heir?"

"I have no answer for that. It would have to be settled by the elected officials or, more likely, by a civil war."

Eleanor told me that she could see why this was such a difficult decision to make.

I didn't mention another fear that I had. I had no idea how I got here and no idea if I would actually die of old age. To outlive all I held dear was a terrible thought and would lead to a stagnant civilization. I would jump from a tower first.

That or disappear and be known as the once and future king. Maybe I was destined to bring the Arthurian legend to life.

These gruesome thoughts aside, I continued my conversation with Eleanor. "The first thing that must be done is to write a constitution. I have an excellent example to share, but this must be done secretly. We are in no hurry, and I want to get it right. Another thing that could be done is to move our fledgling departments to other areas before they get too embedded in Owen-nap."

Over the next several weeks I worked with Thad on deciding how to move the departments of treasury and commerce to London. I took the time to explain to him why I thought this was necessary. That required an in-depth conversation similar to that I had with Eleanor. It also confirmed his position as a senior advisor and key player in our changing government.

While this was going on, the rest of the world didn't sit still. Our efforts to divert the Byzantine Emperor's attention from us by creating problems for him at home backfired. The empire was now in the midst of a civil war after the emperor's assassination.

This civil war encouraged the Arabs to attack Constantinople. So, there was fighting for power inside the city with an ongoing siege on the outside. This disarray allowed the Greeks to rebel successfully. Where it would end up was anyone's guess.

At the radioed pleadings of my banking partners inside Constantinople, I sent five armed schooners to help keep the city harbor open so food could be delivered.

One of the schooner captains realized that the Arabs' supply line was a road along the coast that was within his cannons' range. Two of our ships interdicted this road and broke the Arabs' siege.

§ § § §

The infected Indians fled in every direction but south, spreading smallpox as they went. The civilizations of South America were in complete collapse as there weren't enough people to keep it going. What was once were thriving nations were now tribal groups trying to survive. The need for people broke the practice of human sacrifice.

§ § § §

After many months of construction, they were ready to smelt the first aluminum in Guinea. I had a cargo ship and an armed escort on standby to bring the nuggets to Cornwall.

Eleanor told me I wasn't this worked up when our children were born. I asked her how she would know. She was just lying in bed at the time.

Bad move.

After the dust settled on my bad statement about Eleanor lying in bed while I paced the floor, it only took two days in the doghouse, and things were better. I think Journey had it better during that time. Anyway, my slightly distraught daughter approached me.

"Daddy, will you make me marry some fat old count or baron?"

"Never, what gave you that idea? "

"My girlfriend's marriages are being arranged to those types of men. They say I will have to do the same."

"Your mother and I decided you can marry whomever you want. One of the things I know is that nobility marrying nobility leads to inbreeding. I would rather infuse new blood and keep our descendants strong."

"So, I can marry a stableboy?"

"Not what I would choose, but yes. Who is this is the young man who has won your heart?"

"I would rather not say; he doesn't know it yet."

"All we ask is you think about this young man being your partner in ruling the country. Do you think he meets the same requirements as you do? Not in education but in his intelligence and bearing."

"Oh, I hadn't thought of that. I have to think about it."

After she left, I brought Eleanor up to date on this conversation.

She asked me what we should do about it.

"Since she wouldn't give me his name, I'm going to have all the stableboys investigated."

"Isn't that the abuse of power that you lectured me about not that long ago?"

"*No*! This is a father protecting his daughter".

Eleanor replied with a smirk, "If you say so, dear."

Chapter 24

The reports came back on the stableboys. To say they were discouraging was, to put it mildly. They were stableboys for a reason. They weren't fit for anything else. Ignorant, I could live with. That could be fixed. Stupid, not so much. None of them were smarter than the animals they cared for.

I wasn't looking forward to my next serious conversation with Cathy. It happened quicker than I thought. As I sat pondering the reports, she knocked on the doorframe.

"Daddy, do you have a minute?"

"For you, always."

She advanced with a bounce in her step and a smile on her face. I hated myself for what I was about to do.

"Cathy, about your stableboy."

She got a blank look on her face.

"What stableboy?"

"The one you like."

"Oh, that stableboy. That was to put you off track. He is a baker's apprentice."

Have you ever felt happy and stupid at the same time? It is an interesting feeling. The reports I had been holding had felt like they weighed a ton. Now, they were as light as a feather. I set them on my desk.

As I was doing this, Cathy spoke up.

"I have given serious thought to what you and mother told me what to look for in a life partner. The baker boy isn't it. He is good-looking and fun but doesn't have a serious outlook on life and probably never will."

I heaved a sigh of relief. It was short-lived.

"The only problem is I have little opportunity to meet young men who might meet the standards you outlined. Thinking about it made me realize that you are right. It's just I'm stuck; am I to be an old maid?

This made me laugh.

"I have an idea. Let's find your mother and discuss it with her."

It didn't take long to find her. She was lurking outside my office door. Cathy had spoken to her first.

Eleanor asked, "What is your idea?"

"The upper classes of my time had a ball; it was called a 'coming out ball'. It was a formal announcement that the house's daughter was now an adult and considered to be of marriageable age."

It was a tough sell, but they finally agreed to a ball. Yeah, right, they jumped all over the idea.

I was quizzed for an hour on what that sort of ball consisted of. I had thought of a small affair with maybe a dozen young ladies and some prospective bachelors.

It grew to all young noble ladies of the earldom and all the eligible bachelors. I tried to talk them into finding a way to let our rich merchant class in, but it turned out I had a couple of snobs on hand.

Cathy made the most sense when she pointed out there had to be a limit on how many people were invited, and the purpose was to survey the market of possible husbands.

This didn't sit well with me, as I wanted a way for the two classes to mix. I pointed out that there would be some poor nobleman who would have to be looking out for a rich wife.

The two women agreed with that. So I sprang my next idea on them.

I agreed we should limit this ball, but there is no reason we can't find a way for both classes to mix. In one era of my time, there was a dance held regularly by invitation only. The patronesses of the club could invite whom they pleased. This provided a venue for the nobles and the rich to mix.

They thought this was a wonderful idea. Of course, they both wanted to be patronesses. I had no problem with that. I agreed to underwrite the social club if they agreed to call it "Almack's Assembly Rooms".

Thus, regency society was born a thousand years early. My secret vice was Georgette Heyer.

The only buildings that would be large enough for Lady Catherine's ball were the hall where Eleanor and I got married and several addresses in London.

We decided on London as the best dressmakers were located there, and the most rooms were available for guests. It was hard to figure out what my ladies considered the most important.

Now, there were hundreds of details to work out. The venue, an orchestra, food and drink, a guest list, invitations to be printed, security (my contribution), and many other details.

I remembered an appointment elsewhere and left two ladies to it. My appointment was with a glass of ale in the kitchen. What had I unleashed?

At least they agreed to London, which fell in with my plan to make London the center of my earldom rather than Owen-nap.

At dinner that evening, I was told they would be using people from Thad's staff to do the errands needed for the coming out ball.

Almacks' would be set up by the patrons and patronesses. They had even decided who they would be. Tom Smith and his wife for their contacts in the rich merchants' class and Bart and Liz for their contacts in the up-and-coming trades class.

I was also told they would be developing a budget for me. My job title would be Wallet. That was my thought. Once more, I knew to keep my mouth shut. Since I was perfectly happy with this approach, I smiled and said all the right words.

After dinner, I thought about how the day had progressed from stupid stableboys to grand balls. All in all, I considered it a success. My daughter had a chance to find a suitable life partner. I almost pitied the young men who would be at the ball. They would be like a herd of gazelles surrounded by hungry lions, or lionesses in this case.

It was evil of me, but I was looking forward to watching the event. Being safely married, I was immune to the hunt.

I just thought I was going to be an innocent bystander. The ladies decided that every young lady coming out should be escorted in by one of the bachelors. Since my daughter was high-born, she couldn't be escorted by just any old one.

It would be my job. I was flattered to no end. It would be similar to walking my daughter down the aisle on her wedding day, with less stress. Of course, I couldn't let my ladies know that. I whined a bit but finally yielded.

I did ask what they would do if the numbers didn't work out. That is when I found out that was what the army was for. The army would provide the men or women needed to even out the numbers.

I privately wondered if the troops would get combat pay for this event. Eleanor and Cathy had thought this all out so well that they planned for some of the coming-out girls to be in the military. We allowed recruits to be sixteen or older, which wasn't a surprise. Any noble young men in the service would be joining the ball.

What I thought would be fifty or so youngsters turned into three hundred and some. I was also informed as Commander in Chief of the army I was to issue orders that all those eligible for the ball would be given leave for the event.

I was dragged along to London to give my approval of the building they had selected. It was basically a large open warehouse near the city center. As a building, it was large enough and in a good location.

The problem was it was run down. This was true of the entire area. Here is where I did my bit to make things a success. I bought the main building and all those surrounding it. Next, I had them renovated on an emergency basis. On an emergency basis read that I threw tons of money at the project.

In a month, the builders worked wonders. What was a broken-down area was now prime real estate. When all was said and done, I would make a profit on the project. I didn't need the money, but it felt good to come out on top of things.

The days preceding the ball were a whirlwind of activity. It seems like all my counties had moved to London. There weren't any rooms to be had. Some people opened up their spare bedrooms for rent. Others went to the country and rented out their entire homes. It reminded me of Super Bowl Sunday.

There were parties galore. I skated on as many of them as I could, but in the week preceding the ball, my family would look into as many as three parties a night. That is everyone but Doug. He claimed he was too young for these events. This was from the kid who would sneak off to some forbidden event, such as a boxing match. Doug didn't get away with it. He was to be his mother's escort.

The evening of the actual event was chaos in our house as the ladies got ready. I managed to put on my outfit myself. I had been told what to wear. No simple tux for me, oh no. I had to wear my formal military uniform.

I had mistakenly, at one point in time, listed and described all the medals I had earned in my career with the United States Army. I was surprised when pretty good copies of the medals appeared on my uniform.

There were also campaign medals for the battles that I had been in, here and now. I had those created for my troops, never thinking that I would wear one also. Then, they were the knighthood orders that I was head of. These were stars worn on a sash.

I felt like a fool with all the badges and medals I was wearing, but I was told to get over it. I had earned every one of those. This was true, but I looked like a banana republic dictator.

I wondered if we would take our family coach, which was getting to be shabby-looking. Maybe someone had thought to spruce it up a bit.

When we exited the Tower of London where we were staying, I had a pleasant surprise. No coach awaited us. Instead, a huge black limousine with flags on the front fenders awaited. Sir Bart and Dame Liz were the driver and assistant. The engine purred. They had done a wonderful job.

As we left the Tower, a squadron of cavalry was in front of us and another behind. Troops lined the street the entire two miles of our trip. This was as fancy as anything ever put on for Queen Elizabeth II.

When we arrived, we stepped out on a red carpet. There were movie cameras everywhere. By arrangement, we were the last to arrive. Cathy and I walked down the red carpet arm in arm.

She was interviewed while her picture was snapped hundreds of times. The pictures would be in the papers and the movies in the theater. Every couple at the ball had their presence recorded to be shown in all theaters.

The dance itself was like all other dances. Cathy didn't sit out any of them. The event was for her to meet young men who might make good husbands for her. It didn't take long for me to figure out this wouldn't work.

The boys lining up to ask her to dance were the forward and even pushy ones. They had to form a line, and from the elbowing that was going on, it was a wonder there weren't any fistfights.

This event wasn't bringing out the best. It was bringing forward the worst. At intermission, Cathy confirmed my thoughts.

The next few days were interesting, to say the least. We kept to ourselves in the Tower. The newspapers reported every little detail, scandals and all. There were reports of eleven engagements resulting from the dance. Publicly it was wondered if the earl's daughter had found a match.

Not only was there not a match but there also wasn't any interest. Male callers were turned away at the gate. From a social popularity event, our family was a winner. For identifying a possible husband for my daughter, it was a failure. Privately, as her father, I was a happy man.

Chapter 25

The aftermath of the ball was a time of social upheaval. Our Almacks Assembly Room had instituted monthly dances. All towns of any size, both on our island and the mainland, created their own local assemblies.

The criteria for attending these assemblies varied from town to town. The one common factor was the mixing of the classes. The newspaper reports covered our discussions with Cathy about a future husband. It was reported that a husband had to be a suitable partner rather than a member of your class. We need to start having our family discussions in a SCIF.

This led to many intermixing, usually from one level to the next. Merchant to minor nobility. Minor nobility to higher nobility. Richer to poorer. Most of these matches were well thought out and beneficial to all parties.

The one group that surprised me was the older people of all classes. I thought they would take the attitude that we have always done it this way. Why change? Instead, for the most part, they embraced the change. It seems they were aware of the failings of inbreeding, both biological and class. Previously, they had no way to break free of the social restraints they were working under. Now, they could.

The most common change was the marrying of a rich merchant or their daughter to a minor noble. This raised the merchants to a higher social level and made it possible for the nobles to improve their lot.

The wise ones used the new money to improve their estates, the foolish to gamble it away.

I was happy with this new state of affairs as it strengthened my nation as a whole.

The local papers had a social column where these goings-on were recorded. It also gave rise to several magazines that followed the social events of the day. Cathy couldn't cross the street without it being in the news.

I had to crack a chicken joke. It was the oldest of all. Why did the chicken cross the road? Well, to get to the other side. Unfortunately, I didn't say chicken; I said Cathy. I paid for that one dearly. It took several strands of pearls to settle my ladies down.

Doug listened and learned.

"Dad, I learn from your social mistakes. If you keep going, I will be the smartest man around,"

Smart Alec, if you ask me.

Later, I discovered that Doug was the ratfink who passed my Cathy joke along. He discovered that what warm water poured on your hand when you are asleep will make you do. Juvenile, I know, but even us earls have to have fun.

Cathy herself semi-retreated from the social scene. She gave up her mission to search for her life partner.

She expressed it as, "Whatever will be, will be."

Of course, I had to return with, "Que Sera, Sera". I had to explain it was from another language from my time and meant what she said. I remembered most of the song's lyrics and sang them to her.

My singing voice wasn't great, but it wasn't embarrassing either. The song became a hit within weeks. Cathy made the record. While she wasn't Doris Day, she was pretty good.

This added to her fame and also brought her in contact with the show business set, which was forming as the number of actors and actresses grew. I wasn't thrilled with that as I remembered stories of the

Hollywood crowd. I did what any dad would do. I had each of them investigated and informed Cathy why she should avoid some of them.

I could have forbidden her to associate with them but decided to treat her like an adult and let her make her decisions. It turned out well.

Cathy herself decided to go to college and gain a degree in economics. As the future leader of our country, she would need to understand how things worked. Her mother and I supported this approach.

Our horseless carriage introduced at the ball was a subject followed all over the world. Everyone was looking forward to the time when they would have their own.

To dampen the anticipation, I had Liz show a reporter what had to be done to get that car to the ball. The car was a prototype. Unibodies were a distant dream for us. The body parts normally would have been bolted on. Instead, to make the ball's deadline they had tack welded the pieces together.

A normal road would have shaken the car apart, Since that was not the desired image, the course from the Tower to the ballroom was chosen carefully. It was as smooth as possible. The day before the ball, any potholes were filled in and smoothed over. The car was brought to the Tower on a horse-towed flatbed wagon.

To drive the point home to the reporter, Liz took her for a ride. She chose a bumpy road outside of London. The car didn't make it a quarter mile before it was shedding parts.

The demonstration worked as the story written by the reporter was titled "A Dream to Be."

I had another concern with automobiles. I had previously decided they weren't going to be the common mode of travel. They produced too much pollution and left the countryside paved with asphalt. It also made oil an even more sought-after commodity. I wanted to avoid that if possible.

I didn't know how to do that long-term, but I had a short-term answer. I shifted Bart and Liz's focus from automobiles to military transportation. The emphasis was on diesel-powered trucks, troop carriers, and tanks.

We would need them for our continuing expansion. When we had those vehicles ready for use, I would push them towards the pickup truck or Ute, as my Australian friends called them.

This action plan would prevent Bart and Liz from getting obscenely wealthy in the near term, but in the long term, they would be as rich as Tom Smith.

After the pickup truck would be the articulated lorry or semi-truck as it was called in America.

For some reason, I didn't want to lose all the richness of languages that would never be.

When Bart looked over the drawing of a tank that I had made to give him an idea of what I was talking about, his eyes lit up. We could take the gun turret off, put a large metal blade on the front, and use it to push things. He had invented the bulldozer.

I gave him the go-ahead to work on this as he developed the tank. I also realized that I wouldn't keep the genie in the bottle. I would have to devise another way to avoid internal combustion engine pollution.

I know that electric-powered cars had been looked at as a solution in my time, but the generation of electricity and batteries was only a stopgap as they only moved the problem out of sight.

§ § § §

The plains tribes of North America were almost completely wiped out by smallpox. But the key word was "almost". The survivors had gone in every direction but south. They reached the Pacific coast and spread the disease.

When they reached the tribes in what would have been Illinois and Indiana, the result was the same. The disease was spread as far north as the Inuit. Their lifestyle was on the edge as it was. They were wiped out completely.

From the American Midwest, the disease spread like wildfire throughout the South, only to burn itself out with the Seminoles in Florida. The Caribes on their islands were the only ones unaffected at first. Their downfall occurred when they sent a trading party to the mainland. Again, due to lifestyle, they were destroyed completely.

The message seemed to be, "Cannibalism isn't good for you."

§ § § §

We received news from Timbuktu. Things were going well for them. They were mining salt at an accelerated rate. They could meet our needs for the foreseeable future. They were now self-sufficient in the major crops like wheat and rice.

They did beg for a shipment of coffee as they had run out. This required one of our ships to make a run to Turkey and then to the Niger, where it was moved upstream. This was accomplished in less than a month. I was impressed and hoped no one had died from caffeine withdrawal. I know it would have been close for me.

They did have a minor incursion from an Arab trading party who turned raiders when they saw they couldn't take what they wanted. The Battle of Timbuktu lasted half an hour but was reported at home for days. It was still true, "If it bleeds, it leads."

The governor of Timbuktu sent me a message asking permission to start surveying for a railroad line from Timbuktu to the port at the mouth of the Niger. I was glad to give permission as this would open up territory that hadn't even been opened in my day.

They didn't call it the darkest Africa for no reason. The perpetual rainclouds prevented satellite observation in my time. With the advances being made, they would be able to penetrate the murk in the future, but as of today, this territory is unknown. It could be marked, "Here be monsters, but more likely, here be unknown mineral riches and plants."

That was for the future. I was more interested in the present, particularly the development of dirigibles. The ones we were making weren't anywhere the size of the Hindenburg. We had no reason to haul around a crowd of people and have a piano on board.

We wanted a minimal crew and a bomb load for these first machines. The infrastructure to support this effort was large and expensive. The dirigible couldn't be left out in the weather. Winds would blow the machine all over the place, causing whipsaw damage.

We had to build a hangar large enough to contain the balloon. Since we were building a fleet of ten, I decided on ten separate hangars to spread the risk. These were well separated and had high berms around them. If the gas in a balloon exploded, we didn't want it to spread to the other balloons.

To move the balloons around, we needed ropes from the balloons and firm footing for the men doing the hauling. The balloon would be tethered to a mooring mast. This kept the balloon stable while being loaded from large ramps that reached the loading doors of the balloon. Unlike a blimp, there wasn't a container suspended underneath the envelope. The crew compartments and storage were all within the body of the machine.

The four engines were mounted at the back of the airship. The dirigible's course would be changed by slowing down the engines on one side or speeding them up on the other.

The engines were mounted on a swivel so the dirigible could fly higher or lower. It also meant that it took a long time to change altitude without discharging hydrogen. To land the dirigible from eight thousand feet, the decision had to be made at least eight miles from the landing point.

The hangars were at our home port outside of Owen-nap. Construction was started in Greenland, Jutland, Paris, Monaco, Santander, and Timbuktu. It would take a year to get them all in place. Priority was given to Santander as that would be the base for conquering Spain.

This project was extremely expensive. I had to have more gold coins minted to meet my obligations. I had a concern that once the construction was completed, the increased money supply would lead to inflation.

A conversation with Cathy set that worry aside. From her economics class, an axiom for Cornish economic theory had been developed. It stated that the earl would always find ways to spend money, so inflation wasn't a concern. I didn't know how to take that.

Chapter 26

While testing our dirigibles, an accident or what appeared to be an accident occurred. The fuel feed to the engines shut off, leaving the machine stranded five thousand feet in the air.

The wind was blowing it towards the Channel so the captain ordered hydrogen to be released to bring the ship down. He managed to bring the ship down before it reached the coast.

The lower it got the less the wind was blowing so when it got low enough he released the towing ropes. He had been in radio contact with the ground the entire time so a mounted force was following him.

When the ropes were slowly dragging over the ground, they were seized, and the dirigible was brought under control. The rope was tied to the horses the men had ridden and the aircraft was slowly brought back to its home hangar.

It took two days to move it back. It had taken two hours to go as far as it had.

Once in its hangar, it didn't take the mechanics long to figure out the failure was caused by a fuel switch. The switch had bent when moved into position, freezing it closed. Further investigation proved that the internal steel part had never been hardened.

A check of the inventory of parts for the other dirigibles being produced showed none of these switches had been hardened. There was only one supplier, so it was easy to visit him. He had a small factory near Owen-nap.

The owner claimed the parts had been sent out for hardening. He had receipts to prove that he had paid for them to be hardened. There were no quality records to show that they had been tested upon return or before the completed assembly was shipped.

A visit to the hardening operation was just as disturbing. They had records of the parts being received for hardening but no records that the operation had actually occurred.

The storage shelves for incoming and outgoing parts were next to each other and it would have been easy to ship out a received part without sending it to the hardening operation. Again, there were no quality records of the parts being tested to see if they had been hardened correctly. This was standard practice for the handling of all parts.

There was no evidence of foul play. This was poor management and the lack of a system. I couldn't call it a system failure because there wasn't a system in place, at least by my standards.

Both owners were upset with what happened. No one had made any extra money off of the missing operation.

Thinking about it, I was just as culpable as they were. It had taken the world in my time over a hundred years into the industrial revolution to develop quality systems. I knew about them but had let my industries grow without teaching about quality control.

Dirigible testing was discontinued as I had engineers go through the complete design process of all parts of the aircraft looking for possible single points of failure. Again, no one to blame but me. Thankfully no lives had been lost.

I explained the whole situation to my family. The kids were now old enough to participate in these conversations. Cathy understood what I was telling them. The one that surprised me was Doug.

He was avid in his questioning about good quality practices. Before the end of the evening, I had described the complete ISO 9001:2000.

He thought it was the neatest thing he had ever heard. A way to control things to make them correctly.

I saw a budding quality engineer, or at least an engineer in our family. Since it was one of my loves, I was thrilled, to say the least. Doug and I talked long after Eleanor and Cathy had retired.

He thought it was wonderful there was a way to make things perfectly every time. I had to reel him in and explain that a good system catches mistakes and learns from them so that type of mistake doesn't occur again.

He still didn't get it so I had to explain Murphy's Law to him. "What can go wrong will go wrong at the worst possible time." I also gave him my interpretation of Sod's Law, "Murphy was an optimist."

One point Eleanor made during the evening was that I couldn't beat myself up over this. I was only a man, and there were too many things for me to keep track of everything. She was right. There were too many moving parts to this building of an industrial society and dominating the world for any one person to keep track of things.

The next day I had a meeting with my advisors and explained what happened with the fuel switch but that it was only a symptom of another problem.

After several hours we had a plan. All suppliers to the military would be brought in for an orientation. First, they were given an overview of the ISO Standard and why they would have to put a system in place. There were many objections about the cost as the system would be complex. I tried to explain if they had a simple process then their manufacturing system would be simple.

I used the term manufacturing system to try to correct a basic ISO mistake. The standard wasn't really about a quality system but a manufacturing system. The standard required a quality system to keep the manufacturing system in check and to provide improvement when mistakes were found.

They would be told they had to appoint a quality manager in their factories and a management representative as described in the ISO standard. One person could fill both positions.

The government would be creating a corps of auditors to audit their manufacturing systems to see if they were in place and being used correctly. If they were being used correctly, the owners would see the value of the system as their profits improved. I briefly mentioned Cost of Quality, but it would be covered more in-depth in the management representative and quality manager training.

This effort would take months to implement. To keep our dirigible production moving forward we instituted one hundred percent incoming inspection on all parts for all attributes. This was costly and time-consuming but had to be done.

The redesign project was moving forward. The resulting design would be thirty percent larger than the original machine but would be less failure-prone. Not completely failure-proof as I reminded everyone of the Laws of Murphy and Sod.

Murphy became a saint to the engineers. The engineers would dedicate new designs to Murphy in hopes they would be blessed. Sod was a devil to be avoided at all costs. This was all done in fun, but if I ever heard of worship services, I would put my foot down.

Saint Barbara was the saint of combat engineers and the only one worth a prayer. My company had prayed to her from Normandy to Berlin. She got us through.

While all this was going on, Cathy approached me.

"Dad, do you have a few minutes?"

This was serious, I was Daddy when she was trying to wheedle something out of me. Dad was the sign of a mature conversation. I'm still not ready for my little girl to be mature.

"For you, any time. What's up?"

"There's this boy."

Catching my breath I inquisitively replied, "Yes?"

"His name is Michael. He sits next to me in my economics class. We have been talking for a while. I like him. He is a quite thoughtful person. He has asked me to go to a movie this weekend."

"You don't need my permission to do that."

"I know, but I would like you to allow my guards to stay further away."

My first thought was *hell no*.

"Why do you want them to keep their distance?"

"I like him and don't want to scare him away."

"Do you think he would be scared away? He has to know who you are and that you have bodyguards."

"He does, but it is awkward if he wanted to get closer to me."

My second thought was *hell no*.

"How close were you thinking?"

"Daddy!"

That close. My third thought was *hell no*!

"Have you talked to your mother?"

If I could weasel out of this, I would.

"I did. She said ask you."

Thanks, Eleanor.

The look on my girl's face did me in.

"Okay, the guards can sit further away in the theater but otherwise they will keep their normal stations."

"Oh, Daddy, you are the best!"

As she skipped out of the room, I thought about how much trouble she could get into in a dark movie theater. Oh crap.

I would have an undercover agent sit close to them. If this guy had Roman fingers and Russian hands, I would have him locked away.

It turned out that Cathy and Michael had a nice evening at the movies. They held hands but that was the extent of it.

I expressed my relief to Eleanor who laughed at me.

"He is the dangerous one."

"How could he be dangerous? They only held hands and then went for a milkshake. They didn't even have one shake with two straws."

"How did you court your first wife?"

"We went to the movies, held hands, and had ice cream together."

She smiled at me, "That is why he is dangerous. He is courting her."

"How can we stop this?"

"Why should we?"

"She's too young!"

"And who presented her at a coming out ball announcing to the world that she is of marriageable age?"

"Okay, okay, but I'm having him checked out."

"He comes from a good merchant family and has never been in trouble."

"How do you know this?"

"I had him checked out as soon as he asked her to go to the movie with him."

"So, what do we do?"

"We let nature take its course. They will date and it will get serious or not. As you have said, '*Que sera, sera*.'"

And so, we did. Nothing happened fast, the young couple seemed content to enjoy each other's company and to get to know each other. *Que sera, sera.*

We officially met Michael four months later when Cathy invited him to dinner with us. She had met his parents and now it was his turn.

I was specifically told that I wouldn't be cleaning any firearms that evening. Spoilsports. It turned out Michael was a presentable young man who I instantly liked. He was polite, but not a suck-up like so many people I had to deal with.

The way he looked at, talked to, and treated my daughter told me he was sincere in his affection for her. I asked him what his plans for the future were.

"My Lord, I plan to assist my father in his business."

"What sort of business is that?" I asked, even though I knew all about it down to the last farthing in the cash register. Not that we used farthings.

"We make electronic devices like toasters, radios, and lighting fixtures."

"What would you do in the company?"

"I would like to work on introducing new products to the market. I feel like we haven't scratched the surface of what can be done."

"That sounds interesting and quite a challenge. Also please call me James, or Sir here in the house."

"Yes, sir."

After dinner, he spent some time in the front parlor with Cathy. We avoided the area as we didn't want her to think we were spying on her. The parlor maid outside of the door would fill us in on all the details.

At least I thought so. When I asked her, she saucily told me that Cathy had outbid me. What's a poor father to do? Not even the servants respect him.

After Michael left, Cathy bounced into our sitting room.

"What did you think of him?"

Eleanor and I exchanged looks.

Eleanor told Cathy, "I think we should invite his parents to dinner one evening."

I thought Cathy was too mature to squeal. I thought wrong.

Chapter 27

The reports came in from the investigation at Gibraltar. It was worse than I had feared. The officer corps was thoroughly corrupt. They were selling gunpowder, cartridges, cannons, and rifles to all comers.

This included the Moors, the Basques, and the Byzantines. By our estimates, they had sold five thousand rifles. And twenty cannon. They had kept few records, so we didn't know where they ended up. Murphy would have a field day.

I ordered and led a regiment to Gibraltar to arrest the officers. I had word sent in advance that the regiment would be arriving and was on their way to Africa. They would have two days leave while there.

This would get them ashore without alerting the officers, and I hoped to corner them all before they could run.

The operation worked up to the point of my soldiers arresting the officers. The officers were at their various workplaces around the "Rock". Some surrendered peacefully, some didn't.

Those who were going to fight ordered their men to grab their weapons and defend them. In all cases, they received a rude surprise as the men stood there as the miscreants were seized.

There were a couple of officers who by chance were near a gate to the Spanish side and ran for their lives. It seems the Moors who lived there didn't like them either as their screams were soon cut off.

We had the table of organization of the troops stationed at Gibraltar, so we had extra officers along to fill all those slots.

Once Gibraltar was firmly under the regiment's control a drumhead court martial was held. The evidence of guilt was in hand, so it wasn't a kangaroo court as some countries such as Nazi Germany practiced it. I had directed it to be held in this fashion to cut this cancer out of my army and navy as quickly as possible.

As the evidence was presented, the officers were allowed to make a statement on their own behalf. Most of them took the position that others were doing it, so why shouldn't they? This wasn't a good position because I ordered them to be tied to a post and shot at once.

Only one young ensign was spared. He had reported to duty the previous week as a replacement for a lieutenant who died of drunkenness.

An example was to be set and set it we did. The enlisted men were jubilant. They had known of the wrongdoings but were unable to do anything about it. They would have been killed if they had said anything.

I was asked why they didn't send letters back to Cornwall to inform headquarters what was going on. The response was, why should they have trusted anybody?

Five senior enlisted men were brought to my headquarters by a contingent of soldiers. These senior men were collaborating with the officers.

Nothing is straightforward and easy in a situation like this. There were the families of the dead officers to take care of. Some of the wives were probably in on it with their husbands; others would know nothing. There were children involved.

There was a bank on Gibraltar that the officers used. Most had large accounts. Those who didn't were known gamblers. These accounts were seized.

Not wanting to be seen as a total monster, I gave the wives a choice. If they had family in Cornwall who would take them in, they and their children could go there. Their belongings, including household items, would be shipped with them.

This took care of the majority of the officers' families. I did not doubt that many of them had large sums of money hidden in their goods. I had ordered they were not to be searched.

I wanted them to settle into a quiet life in Cornwall, not a life of destitution. Some of them may have earned it, but I didn't want the bad publicity that went with it. Even though I wasn't the bad guy in the story, the muckrakers would find a way to make me look bad.

Four women had nowhere to go. I didn't know what to do with them or their children. I had them brought to me and asked them what I should do.

The answer surprised me.

The oldest lady was their spokesperson. "My Lord, between us we have some money set aside. We would like to stay here as Gibraltar has become our home. We would like to open an inn. There is a shortage of such here and we think we could make a living doing this."

I love problems that solve themselves. I gave my permission. I also made certain they had partnership papers drawn up. These were spouses of thieves, and they had a "little" money. I didn't want a problem with their partnership at a later date.

I also made certain the commandant kept an eye on them to make certain that an honest inn was being run. No telling what mischief could occur.

All of these events were broadcast back home. Public opinion was that I had handled things as well as I could.

As one announcer said, "Our earl is showing a surprising maturity for his age. I knew him when he was a young man. He was impulsive in his decisions, to say the least. You might have called him a hothead."

He went on, "The turning point in his life appears to be when he almost died from a fall from his horse. He was in a coma for days, and when he awakened, he was a changed man. He was showing more maturity overnight. Since then, he has grown in his outlook on the world and the wisdom of his decisions. If one didn't know better, one would think he was a fifty-year-old man rather than one approaching thirty."

Eleanor and I had a good laugh at that. It was more like the maturity of a one-hundred-year-old man.

Once Gibraltar was under control, Eleanor and I returned to Owen-nap. Several issues were waiting for us there. The most pressing was to meet Cathy's boyfriend's parents. It was a pressing issue because Cathy insisted it was.

They were invited for dinner with us in the keep. We wanted it to be private rather than broadcast to the whole world.

It is a good thing that we did. Mike was a good kid and well-behaved. I don't know if it was nerves that had Mike's mom a talkative wreck. She wouldn't shut up.

Name-dropping at every chance she could, she also proved she was an avid reader of the scandal sheets. According to her, everything she read was gospel.

Poor Cathy and Mike were cringing every time she opened her mouth. Mike's dad didn't try to compete with her. Instead, he ignored everything she said. He was more interested in what he could get from me.

In no uncertain terms, he let me know that he expected a huge dowry from me for Cathy. This would include special treatment on any contracts that he might bid on, not only now, but forever.

He came across as a slimy jerk as he described how he kept his costs down in manufacturing. If nothing else, he earned tax, safety, and quality audits.

Eleanor and I kept our feelings to ourselves during dinner but cut the evening as short as possible. Poor Cathy turned to her mother and fell into her arms crying as soon as they left.

The one I felt sorry for was Mike. He hadn't come across like his parents at all. During dinner, you could tell he was totally mortified.

The next day was even worse. Mike's Dad was bragging in all the merchant's coffee houses that he had a permanent connection with me and that they would have to seek his favor if they wanted any government orders in the future.

Talk about counting your chickens before the eggs are hatched. These eggs haven't even been laid yet.

Eleanor, Cathy, and I had a long talk. The upshot was that we didn't disapprove of Mike. At the same time, there was no way that we would associate with his parents. Mike had a choice to make. Cathy or his parents.

It occurred to me that they could have an accident, but that wasn't how I wanted to operate. On a national level, it was war, and all was fair. On a personal level, I had to conform to the norms of society.

Cathy would have a talk with Mike and see how it went. She agreed with us about his parents. When she had dinner with them, Mike's mom talked a lot but not over much. We could put that down to nerves. Mike's father's actions were beyond the pale.

I held off on ordering any investigations on the dad's business. Cathy and Mike's talks would determine how fast and how hard my actions would be. There would be an investigation no matter the outcome of their relationship.

At least that was my plan. The Bank of Cornwall wanted to know if what Mike's dad had told them was true. He was applying for a large loan and told them that I would be guaranteeing it.

You can imagine how quick and terse my answer was. I had Mike's dad, John, arrested on attempted fraud charges. Things had gone too far.

John's lawyer sent word that unless I dropped all charges, John would withhold his permission for Mike to marry Cathy.

This was a moot point as Mike and Cathy were just getting to know each other, and Mike hadn't asked Cathy to marry him.

Stories as sordid as this always got out. I think the mother found her chance to get into the scandal sheets she was always talking about. She gave an interview telling how we were snobs and didn't even extend them the basic courtesies.

Poor Cathy was beside herself. All she wanted was a boyfriend who she could get to know. She didn't want to be the center of this mess. She also was getting a better understanding of why we checked on the background of any boy she was interested in.

While this drama was playing out, world events were proceeding. The Greeks were in complete rebellion against the Byzantine Empire.

The Byzantine army had returned to defend Constantinople. Since the Arabs had retreated from sieging the city walls, it was more like the generals wanted in on the power grabs that were going on. For all practical purposes, Greece was now an independent country.

I thought about annexing them, but they would be too far from us to provide better support. I did send a contingent to open diplomatic relations with them.

It was no surprise that they demanded in return for their recognition that we provide troops and ships for their defense for when the Byzantines got their internal issues settled.

I was getting tired of all these demands both on a personal and national level. I was the one with the hammer and was about to lower it.

The wonderful thing about radio is that you can keep in contact in real time. After my people were back on board the schooner they arrived on, I had them send a note to the Greek leaders.

The note told them that since they were unreasonable in their demands, we wished them the best but wouldn't be helping them remain independent. The schooner cast off as soon as the note was sent.

The Greek leaders must have been waiting for it, as the schooner was under catapult fire as it left the harbor. The schooner's captain returned the salute in the same manner it was given. One cannon shot destroyed the catapult.

We found out later that the leaders of the Greek rebellion had been standing at the catapult to see us run with our tails between our legs. New, more reasonable leaders were soon in place, and they sent me gifts to soften my attitude.

I had read something about Greeks bearing gifts.

Chapter 28

With a territory as large as mine there was always something happening that demanded my attention. While the Greeks were busy with their rebellion, I was looking to the west.

The native American Indians who had come from Iceland had learned to speak Cornish. I did realize there was a problem with what I thought of the natives of North America. One, there wasn't an America, two Columbus thought he had found India so called them Indians. They weren't.

That only left natives which was too generic; we were all natives of someplace or the other.

I asked him what he called the large land mass he came from.

"I call it North America, the same as you. We natives didn't have a name for the entire land mass. Until I saw one of your maps, I had no idea how large it is."

Ok, so I had called the two land masses North and South America in public, which in turn made the news. Thus, Amerigo Vespucci's and Martin Waldseemüller's errors were continued in a different time.

To confound things, he told me his people were Iroquois while generally they were called Indians. Okay, Chris, I continued your mistaken identity. So, Tokala, or Fox, in Cornish, was a native American Indian. Somedays I get a headache from thinking about things.

Fox and I had several long conversations about what would happen when our two cultures encountered each other. The Iroquois were a hunter-gatherer society with only light agriculture, and ours an agricultural one. We both agreed it wouldn't be good.

That in itself wasn't the problem; it was the question of land ownership. His people didn't recognize ownership of land in specific parcels but did consider land that they could defend as belonging to the entire tribe.

I asked him if it would be possible for a treaty between our two groups. We would guarantee the territory they controlled, and they would allow us to survey the land and deed it to the tribe who could share it with their people. To work they would have to shift to an agricultural society.

We would have to teach them how to farm and provide them with start-up implements. If they did this they wouldn't starve in a bad winter as many of them did.

Fox was the one who brought up the starvation point. He had seen our farms and how productive they were. He wanted the benefits for his people.

He was just another warrior of the Iroquois so had no special status with the tribe. He would be willing to go with a group of our men to open negotiations. Part of these would be to invite a group of their leaders back to Cornwall to see what we had accomplished.

He agreed enthusiastically. His people would benefit, and he would gain great status with his people. I also made a point that we had a terrible disease called smallpox and his people would have to be vaccinated against it. He proudly showed me his lightning bolts where he had received his.

I turned it over to the army to arrange an expedition to the new world. They would take plenty of gifts in the form of tools, mirrors, necklaces, knives, and different spices. No firearms were to be given out.

Fox was to be accompanied by one hundred troops and a surveying team. I hoped they would be able to demonstrate how we laid out land.

There was also an official photographer to record events. The newspaper asked to embed a reporter and I gave the okay. I did insist the reporter have field experience. This would be no trip for amateurs.

I was woken from a sound sleep two nights later. We had a brigade of five hundred men under attack in a mountain pass while they were traveling through the Basque-controlled Pyrenees.

They were pinned down by a large force with rifles. The trap had been sprung early so they had time to hunker down in the rocks lining the pass. Normally, they would have charged into the ambush, but the Basque were high up the mountain side and they would have been picked off before they could come to grips with the enemy.

I wished we could execute those corrupt officers at Gibraltar a second time. This battalion of five hundred men was an advance force to start a build-up to fight the Moors. They were traveling light as they would soon be followed by a wagon train.

The wagon train was out of contact, and I feared it was lost. This meant the enemy now had more ammunition than the trapped soldiers.

There were no other troops close enough to reinforce the brigade in time. The soldiers only had water in their canteens, so they had three days at the most to get out of the trap.

I wracked my brain about what could be done. That was when I noticed buzzing out in the night. It was the sound of a dirigible going through flight testing.

That was it. The airships hadn't been on any long-distance flights, but we had no reason to think they couldn't do it.

From our radio room, I ordered the dirigible to be loaded with two of our new fuel-air bombs, along with two-hundred-and-fifty-gallon water buffaloes. The balloon was rated to lift forty thousand pounds, which gave us plenty of weight to play with. The rest of the load was to be ammunition and rations.

All the activity woke Eleanor up, and she saw me off. She didn't like it but knew I had to go on this trip. It was a two-hour horseback ride to the dirigible's base, and they were busy loading the aircraft as I arrived.

In the flight officers' shack, I found the pilot and the co-pilot plotting a course. It would be directly across the channel to spend as little time over water as possible. The trip was close to eight hundred miles. With the prevailing winds we could make sixty miles an hour so planned thirteen hours en route.

They finished loading in another hour, and we lifted off. I found an empty crew bunk so crawled in to finish my night's sleep. I will deny forever that I had any thoughts about Eleanor and the mile-high club.

I managed another four hours sleep. That put us somewhere over France. We were following an old pilot's method of navigation. That is, we were following railroad tracks south.

I was given an update on the brigade's situation. They were sitting tight. They were taking casualties but not disastrously so. The Basque were content to keep them pinned down. It appeared they planned to force the brigade to surrender.

This would give the Basque another five hundred rifles with little effort on their part. I agreed with their strategy but damned them anyway. I thought about ordering the executed officers dug up and rehanged. It was terrible not being able to take any immediate direct action.

The clock finally ticked down and we found the mountain pass where our troops were pinned down. It was touch and go but they guided us in by the sound of our engines.

At seven hundred feet above the mountain pass we were safe from ground gunfire. The pilot circled the Basque positions. From the muzzle flashes, we could tell they were firing at us, but the bullets would expend their energy before reaching our height. They were in more danger from their own fire as they were shooting straight up. Apparently, a Basque officer caught on because the gunfire died out.

The pilot and I had a conversation about how to drop the bombs. Normally we would let them float down on parachutes and set the bomb off by a radio signal. The winds in the mountain pass were swirling so bad that we couldn't be certain where they would land. We decided it would be best if we let gravity do its job.

It would take timing on our part to send the radio signal to get an airburst, but it would be the safest for our troops on the ground. It became a question of depth perception. The dirigible crew had all been tested for their eyesight and there was one young air crewman that had better depth perception than the rest of us.

I know that mine was deteriorating with time. This was too important to leave to my ego. We wanted the best to do the job.

The pilot positioned the dirigible over the west side of the pass immediately above the Basque troops. He had us flying into the wind and slowed the engines down until we were station-keeping.

Our young bombardier ordered the release of the first bomb. It seemed to fall forever. I thought for certain he was leaving it too late. He wasn't. When he pushed the button to ignite the bomb, there was an enormous flash. It bounced our balloon around so bad I thought it would fall apart.

When the smoke cleared, nothing was moving on that mountainside. The pilot then directed the airship to the other side of the pass.

The Basque troops there had seen what had just happened across from them and were abandoning their positions. Unfortunately for them, they had to squeeze through a narrow opening to flee. Our second bomb caught them bunched up. This time we could see charred remains.

We circled the battlefield at a lower height but attracted no gunfire. The brigade down below sent troops out to ensure the area was clear. After an hour of loitering over the pass, we were given clearance to bring the aircraft down.

With the winds, it was a tricky job but our pilot was able to get us low enough that the ropes could be released. The soldiers on the ground seized them and pulled us down. The ropes were tied off on the many boulders littering the area.

The dirigible had been designed with this sort of event in mind. There was a large cargo door from which a long ramp could be extended the remaining five feet to the ground. The ship was unloaded as fast as possible and reloaded with the brigades' casualties.

We were concerned with a stray gust of wind forcing the dirigible down and tearing the body open.

The machine was unloaded and reloaded in what had to be record time, but since this was the first time it had been done it was a record no matter what.

There were fourteen dead from the brigade and twenty-seven wounded. Once they were on board, we started the trip back to Cornwall. The brigade had sent two medical corpsmen with us so the wounded had care on the return trip.

Even though we had rescued the brigade and destroyed the Basque, it was a miserable trip with the cries of the wounded and the associated smells.

I thought the trip out had seemed long. This was beyond forever.

In transit, we got a report from the brigade. They had scoured the Basques' positions. Their best estimate was a thousand Basques killed. That was from the number of burned and melted rifles found. The bodies were impossible to count as they were in many pieces.

I would have to have a staff meeting when I got back to Owen-nap. We had a treaty with the Basque and they had broken it to a fare thee well.

I suspect they would be eager to sue for peace when they saw the results of their ambush. We could destroy any of their villages from the air. I was tempted to do that to send a message but remembered that there were women and children in those towns.

They shouldn't have to pay a price for their leaders' stupidity. Now if I could get their leadership to gather in one spot....

Chapter 29

Setting the Basque situation aside for the moment, I called a meeting of my military advisors. It was time to plan our invasion of Hispaniola or Spain as I knew it.

Our mission statement was simple: remove the African Moorish invaders and incorporate the territory into Greater Cornwall. I didn't use the term; one of my advisors did as a shorthand method of describing our holdings. It worked for now.

The first decision was a simple one. We had to stop the Moors from bringing in any more troops or settlers. That required a coastal blockade of ships coming into Spain. We would inspect the ships, and those with Moorish settlers would be turned back; those with troops would be interned.

From past encounters, we knew most of the Moorish ships would surrender easily. The ships with settlers were only lightly armed with small catapults and had given in easily.

The ships with Moorish troops would be a different kettle of fish. Some would surrender and some choose to fight. Even the fights would come in two types. Some of the captains fired their catapults once, away from us.

Like the British Navy of the nineteenth century, they then could claim they surrendered after a fight.

Several of the Moorish ships would choose to have a real sea battle. Every time these would be settled quickly by our cannons. It was a shame, but those ships invariably lost a lot of men before lowering their flags. Cannons vs. catapults wasn't a fight, it was a slaughter.

Once the ships surrendered, we had to decide what to do with the Moorish soldiers. To intern troops meant we had to set up a camp to hold them.

Near Gibraltar made the most sense. There would be the logistics of supporting such a camp. Someone suggested shipping them to Guinea to work our mines. That actually was a good idea, and we went for that.

It would be easier to support a camp in Guinea where the interned troops couldn't obtain any outside support and it gave us additional labor to mine bauxite. I was all for that.

After discussing the details of a blockade, we decided we didn't have enough ships for complete containment. We would detail some of our small fleet to guard the long Spanish coast but would take the blockade closer to their home.

We would shut down their major ports. We had the ports spied out and found that most of their troops were boarded at Tangiers which made sense as it was the shortest trip from North Africa to Spain. It was especially convenient as my traitorous officers at Gibraltar had been helping them.

The settlers were coming from Badis, Oran, and Algeria. These were small ports and easy to blockade. We would stop all ships. If they weren't loaded with settlers they were allowed to proceed. Those with settlers were turned back.

We soon had the impression that after the first few ships were turned, the only reason they were even trying was that their captains were collecting payment for the trip, knowing full well they wouldn't be making it.

I ordered that any ship stopped twice was to be impounded. The settlers were sent back ashore near their point of departure. The ships were sent on to Guinea to be dismantled. We could always use building materials and more labor for the mines.

Tangiers proved to be a tougher harbor. We could capture ships once they left the harbor, but it was too well-defended to sail into it. Once the Moors realized that we were impounding their ships, they quit sailing.

Over a hundred ships were sitting in the harbor, bottled up, but ready to sail as soon as we left the harbor unguarded.

Rather than spend years sailing back and forth in front of the harbor as the British did to Napoleon, my advisors recommended that we destroy the ships in harbor.

Since it would be too costly to send our ships in, we decided to use our dirigibles. We now had five operational airships, so we sent them with two of the fuel-air bombs each to Tangiers.

Our spies in the port reported that most of the ships were sitting empty. Only a few had watchkeeping sailors on board. Knowing this, we ordered the dirigibles to buzz the ships once to warn the watchkeepers that we were there.

That part of the plan was about half successful as the spies later reported that some watchkeepers abandoned ship, while most stayed aboard.

That was the watchkeeper's last mistake as the five airships returned and dropped their deadly load. We had planned on bombs for two passes. The second pass wasn't needed as the dirigibles could see that all ships in the harbor were burning.

Our contingency plans allowed for this. The dirigibles then proceeded to buzz the huge army camp outside of the city. The troops in the camp were smart enough to run for their lives. It only took two of our bombs to destroy the encampment and all of the supplies stacked there.

The last three bombs were used to set fire to the fields that were used for grazing their calvary horses. The horses were the smartest of all. As soon as the dirigibles flew over them, they stampeded to safety.

With no ships, soldiers with no housing or supplies, and no fodder for their horses, the assembled army had to be disbanded. At that point, we declared our blockade a success which freed up our small navy for other tasks. We did send a dirigible to fly up and down the North African coast to keep track of any new developments.

There were no new attempts to send either troops or settlers to Spain, so we had cut off the existing Moorish armies in Spain. Now we were ready for our next steps in our battle plan.

While we had been stopping any additional troops and settlers arriving, we had been active on several other portions of our plan.

We needed to know how many soldiers the Moors now had. Their army wasn't concentrated in one neat package for us. Our rough guess was that they had two hundred and fifty thousand men available.

These couldn't be kept together for several reasons. The most important was that they had no way of feeding that many men at once. The army had to be spread out across Spain just to feed them.

The second reason was that they had to occupy the major cities and towns so they wouldn't start raiding the Moors' supply lines.

Our goal was to lure the Moorish army back together and defeat them. If that didn't work, we would defeat them in detail by taking each city as we came to them. The Moorish leader Tariq would be a fool to let that happen.

To find out where and how many Moors we had to face, spies had been sent out to the major cities. Before entering each city, they hid radio equipment. The antenna for each unit was a long copper wire that could be run up a tree, or if needed, tied to a balloon filled with hydrogen.

Trees were the preferred method as the spies could only carry so many balloons and a canister of hydrogen under pressure. They would only get five transmissions this way so the copper wire up a tall tree would be best.

It took three months before the spies were able to report back on all the cities. The Moors would be able to field an army of three hundred thousand men. The troops were evenly distributed across Spain. Any uprising would have failed.

Now that we knew what we were facing, we had to choose a battlefield and a way to get the Moors there.

When the Moors saw us taking their newly conquered cities one by one they would assemble their army and come after us.

Scouting with our dirigibles, we decided that we wanted to have the battle near Toledo.

The Tajo River, Tarus in modern Spain, ran east to west and was the longest river in Spain. The river Jarama merges with the Tajo near Toledo. An army following us along the Tajo would have to enter a series of passes. They led to a Y formed by the merging of the Tajo and Jarama.

There was no practical way for an army to circle us. They would have to follow us into the mouth of the Y.

We flew teams to the proposed battle site to prepare the field. We planned to have troops on either side of the Y across the two rivers. That and a following blocking force would seal the Moorish army into the mouth of the Y, and we would turn it into a killing field.

There could be no offers for surrender to an army of this size. If they surrendered there was no way for us to maintain control if they decided to revolt.

At the confluence of the two rivers, we set our trap. On the far bank of each river, we built firing platforms. These platforms were concealed from across the river. Our men could step up onto the platform and shoot down onto the men across the river. If a man was wounded or needed a moment to rest, he could step back and down, and he would be hidden from enemy fire.

A Moorish archer might arc a shot over the platform and hit one of our men, but it would be dumb luck.

Interspersed along the row of firing platforms were batteries of cannon. Like any other ambush of this sort, we had to be careful about hitting our men across from us. Since we would be firing down on the Moors, this shouldn't be a problem.

Behind the firing platforms, MASH units and field kitchens were set up. There was no way to predict how long this fight could last. It might be several days or be over in minutes.

To bring the Moors to our battlefield, we carefully planned an advance. Starting from Santander, we planned to march on Pamplona. Then we would turn south towards Burgos.

We would then head west to take Tudela. East to Zaragoza. Then west towards Toledo. Our spies would let us know the progress being made by the Moorish army. We would speed up or slow down as appropriate.

The object was to enter the narrow pass heading to Toledo before the Moors.

We had closed off the mountain pass a week before our arrival. Any who entered the pass were captured and held. All those who lived inside our zone of control were moved to safety. For their safety from the battle and our safety from anyone letting the Moors know what waited for them.

We had observation balloons looking down on the mountain pass, so we knew where they were at all times. The balloons were high up and at least five miles beyond the pass so no one on the ground in the pass could see them.

Our largest concern was that the Moors had bought rifles and cannon from Gibraltar. If the weapons were in a concentration of troops, they could be a powerful force. If they were spread out, then it would be easier to defeat them.

The Moors had assembled their army to the south and east of us, marching their army hard to cut us off from entering the pass to Toledo.

We had it timed well and were safely in and through the narrow parts of the pass.

The three hundred thousand Moors were following our force of twenty thousand men into the pass. Unbeknownst to them, after their entire army entered the pass, we had another ten thousand men coming in behind them to put a plug in the funnel.

Yet another twenty thousand men were waiting at the battle site. One thing I was glad of—the huge Moorish army had outrun their camp followers so no women and children would be involved in the battle.

Chapter 30

All was going to plan as the Moors entered the pass to Toledo. Their entire force was inside the pass and stretched out over five miles when the wheels fell off my plan.

My rear guard that was to bottle up the Moors got too far ahead of themselves and was spotted by the Moors.

The Moors immediately turned and attacked our rearguard. The only thing that saved them was that the Moors were limited as to the number of troops that they could bring to bear in that narrow pass.

My rear guard had cannon which they used quickly. The Moors backed off as the mouth of that pass became filled with their bodies. There were too many Moors for my men to advance and too much firepower for the Moors to break out. It was an impasse.

We would win this battle as the Moors were lacking water in the dry pass. They would get desperate and try to break out. It would be costly for both sides.

Since my trap at the confluence of the rivers was no longer valid, my generals and I decided to move our troops up to the Moors vanguard.

We would have them trapped between two forces. Unfortunately, the blocking force would be twenty thousand men and the force in the valley thirty thousand. It would have been better if it was reversed.

Someone suggested we bring the dirigibles in and slaughter the Moors. That had been the original plan. Now I was sickened at the thought of killing so many young men far from home.

Instead, I ordered four dirigibles, two on each side of the mountain pass, to drop bombs on the mountain top. I hoped to intimidate the Moors into surrendering.

Our fifth dirigible was stationed over the Moors high enough they couldn't reach it, even with rifle fire. Using loudspeakers, we informed them in their language of what they were about to see.

When the fuel-air bombs went off, they were an unholy sight to see. Flames and thunder rolled over the mountain pass.

Once the dust and noise had settled, it was broadcast to those on the ground that the next bombs would be dropped on them. To avoid this, they were to lay down their weapons and march deeper into the valley.

One thing worked out well. All the senior leadership of the Moors had been killed in the original battle at the mouth of the Y. The men surrendered.

Deeper in the valley, our forces were in two groups. The first was comprised of ten thousand men and their mission was to ensure that the Moors were disarmed. We weren't worried about small knives hidden on them. It was swords, spears, bows, and firearms we were after.

It took two days to process the Moors through our lines. We did bring up food and water to them to avoid riots. Once the Moors passed the first line, our rear guard moved up. We now had the Moors detained between two thirty-thousand-man armies.

Now the question was what to do with them. My original plan was to kill most of them in battle so I wouldn't be facing this exact problem.

That was when I remembered Janissaries. The Janissaries were a standing army created by a Turkish sultan. They were the first standing army in the world. Until then all troops were levied from the local population or from nobles who owed fealty to the country's leader.

The sultan used Christian slaves who he forcibly converted to Islam. They were circumcised which at the time separated them from Christianity.

They were paid well and only answered to the sultan. They were the most loyal troops of the time. There was nowhere else they could go.

I would hire all these soldiers to be my standing army. Like others of our time, troops were called up at need.

The Janissaries would be allowed to marry and follow their religion. Islam hadn't been founded yet in this timeline, and if I had my way it would never come into existence. There were many good Muslims, but since they had no central leadership, any local bozo could cause trouble. At least the Catholics had a centralized system that kept their extremists under control.

Bringing this army under my control while providing housing and food would be an enormous and expensive task.

One thing for certain was that I couldn't let this army sit around. They had to be out there doing something. That meant war. What had I gotten myself into?

It would mean almost a million meals a day! We had brought in a lot of food in case of an extended campaign but nothing like what we would need.

I had another thought. I wasn't going to force these men into my army. It would be better if most of them chose to go home. I had an announcement made in their camp that night. They would be asked tomorrow if they wanted to stay and join my army as full-time paid soldiers or be shipped home.

The next day we made it simple. If they wanted to go home, they were to go to the south side of the pass. Those who wanted to join my army moved to the north.

I heaved a sigh of relief when a huge majority of them chose to go home. Fewer than thirty thousand were staying. That we could handle.

Those who wanted to stay were the younger troops. Older married men wanted to return to their families.

There were enough senior sergeants in the mix to leave us with an intact chain of command that fit their style.

Now all that remained was to move the bulk of the Moors back to a port and ship them home. We used Gibraltar as the debarkation port back to Tangiers. The Moors didn't have enough ships, but we did. It took us a month with each ship crossing the strait twice a day, but we made it happen.

The Tangier authorities complained bitterly about us overwhelming their resources. One of my men jokingly offered to dump the returnees overboard. The Moorish officer thought that a wonderful idea. My man backed off of that idea quickly.

We did ship some excess food supplies to Tangiers as they were having a hard time feeding everyone. Even with soldiers leaving for their homes every day they were stretched thin.

We hadn't returned any of their weapons so the soldiers couldn't get up to too much mischief.

The Moors that remained with us were broken up into five-thousand-man groups. There were six of these groups. We moved them to areas twenty to thirty miles apart. We didn't want too many of them together.

Once we had them settled, the training began to make them soldiers rather than warriors. A thousand of my men were the trainers of each group. Since my people had firearms, they could head off any trouble.

Our fears proved groundless as the Moors took to being soldiers like ducks to water. Maybe regular meals, regular pay, and good housing had something to do with it.

We helped to get messages back to families in North Africa that the men were alive and well.

Once the Moors were trained in the basics of soldiering, including firearms, I intended to have them rotated through Cornwall so they could see how we lived. This would seal the deal with them.

The bulk of my men in Spain were distributed in villages around the country. Larger towns had their own MASH unit stationed there.

Smaller ones had visiting units. Our MASH corps was getting to be as large as an army. At my suggestion, they adopted the motto of, "Blood and Thunder".

I explained it came from a unit similar to theirs that I had read about. The ladies loved it. Before they had been treated as weak women. Now they were looked at as fighters. As they should; they were present on every battlefield.

Once things were settled down, I headed back to Cornwall for a joyous reunion with my wife and children.

My little empire had grown once more. It was time for a new title. The simple thing was to promote myself to duke and absorb Spain into Cornwall.

A concern that I had was that my eggs were all in one basket. I was setting up a government in Cornwall which should work. However, if things went wrong, like a civil war, I could lose everything.

After hours of discussion with Eleanor and Cathy, I decided to call myself Duke of Hispaniola and Earl of the Marches of Cornwall. They would be two separate countries under my control.

That meant I would have two armies, one in Cornwall and the other in Spain. I couldn't help myself. It was Spain and would always be Spain to me.

Our family conversations also included the fact that I intended to conquer Europe to start with. Cathy told me I was silly. It was obvious that I was going to rule the world. She wasn't wrong. How else could I ensure the well-being of me and mine?

Of course, this gave her the opportunity to tell me to get on with it. The sooner I made king, the sooner she would be a princess. Kids!

The end of Book 5 Cast in Time

Backmatter

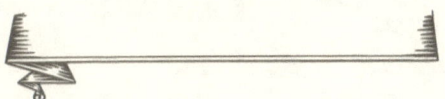

C oming soon Book 6: Duke
        Check out my website *enelsonauthor.com[1] and sign up for my newsletter.

FOR INFORMATION ON hiring Janet E. Rupert to edit your fiction project, email:

janeteditorrupert@gmail.com

---

1.   https://enelsonauthor.com/

Other books by Ed Nelson

The Richard Jackson Saga

Book 1: The Beginning
Book 2: Schooldays
Book 3: Hollywood
Book 4: In the Movies
Book 5: Star to Deckhand
Book 6: Surfing Dude
Book 7: Third Time is a Charm
Book 8: Oxford University
Book 9: Cold War
Book 10: Taking Care of Business
Book 11: Interesting Times
Book 12: Escape from Siberia
Book 13: Regicide
Book 14: What's Under, Down Under?
Book 15: The Lunar Kingdom
Book 16: First Steps

In The Richard Jackson World

Mary, Mary
More Mary

Stand Alone Story

Ever and Always

The Cast in Time series

Book 1: Baron
Book 2: Baron of the Middle Counties
Book 3: Count
Book 4: Earl
Book 5: Earl of the Marches